AWAKEN PERSEPHONE

BY HOLLEY LUNSFORD

Library of Congress Cataloging-in-Publication Data available
ISBN 979-8-9938107-1-3

Printed in the United States of America

For the women who have planted the seeds of strength, courage, and love in my life…

This is for you.

TABLE OF CONTENTS

PROLOGUE

When I first began to fade, it felt like a tickle in the back of my throat. The tickle gradually became an itch and spread from my throat to my mouth, from my mouth to my face, from my face to my chest, and so on until the itch consumed every part of me. The itch then became an ache, and when that turned into numbness, I knew I would soon be gone.

I already knew that the fade was coming for me because I was one of the last of us left. I can't imagine why I remained so much longer than the others.

The fade had started with my father and had been

a great shock to us all. It was slow to arrive, but in hindsight I could see that the signs of its coming had been there for ages. First, he'd forgotten his own name. He forgot his job. He forgot all his children. His wives, his lovers, his friends. All of us were wiped from his mind, one by one. For years, he would look at us with confusion in his eyes, bewilderment and frustration corrupting his face.

At first, we offered him all the help we could. We tried everything to stop his obvious decline, without ever even knowing what we were up against.

And then one day he was just gone.

After that, it became obvious what had happened to him, but it was far too late to stop it from happening to the rest of us.

My father took the longest to fade, and I could never decide if I should feel grateful for that or not. I suppose that, in the end, it doesn't matter.

When I felt the fade start to happen to me, my husband took my face in his hands and stared deeply into my eyes. He told me that he loved me. That he always would. We kissed. I never told him, but deep down I was grateful to be leaving first. My mother had already faded, and I couldn't bear the thought of losing him, too, and being left alone in the world.

His eyes, black as a moonless night and full of sorrow, were the last thing my eyes saw.

And then, I was floating in a warm sea of black.

CHAPTER ONE

Three months until my eighteenth birthday, and I still have absolutely no idea what I'm going to do with my life.

I know it may seem like a silly thing to say, but I feel like I'm the only person I know who has literally no direction for the future. We still have a little over nine weeks in the school year, and I've already been accepted into a couple of the colleges I've applied for. I guess that's comforting, but still. If I ever want to get out of this little blip of a nothing town, I need a plan.

My mom, obviously, would prefer me to go to

Edgecreek State University—a mere forty minutes away—so I can live at home and commute. She also thinks I should major in dentistry because of one comment I made when I was six; I told our dentist that I wanted to be like him when I grew up.

I know I shouldn't get so irritated by the fact that she wants to keep me close. I know she means well, and she only wants what's best for me. I know that I should be more understanding, but I can't help feeling like she should also be more understanding of me and what I want for my future.

I also know I shouldn't be quite so testy about the whole dentistry thing but come *on*. I get wanting your kid to go into a secure sort of career—I mean, people are always going to need a dentist, right? But she talks to anyone who will listen about *my* dream of being a dentist, *my* ambitions, blah, blah, blah. Even though I have never expressed any real interest in it outside of that *one* comment.

To be fair, I've also never exactly shot the dentist idea down when *she* relentlessly brought it up.

Nor have I ever shared with her anything that I actually might *want* to do.

All that changes now, right this very instant.

She's driving me to school, and I sit in the passenger's seat mentally replaying one last time the little speech I've prepared: *Mom, I was thinking I'd like to major in music or music business next year. No, I never* actually *said I wanted to be a dentist, and I don't. I hope you can support and respect my* actual *dreams.*

I take a deep breath in and—

Nothing.

I look at my mom, who is totally zeroed in on the road in front of her, and notice her long brown hair has thick, wiry grays streaking through it. How did those get there? When did she develop crow's feet? When did her mouth start looking like a perpetual frown?

A couple of years ago, my mom was never *not* laughing. All traces of that Tracy are gone, and now there's just a hollowed-out husk of her driving me to school with glazed eyes that are still red from crying in

6

the shower this morning because she thought I couldn't hear her in there.

I always hear you, Mom.

The car slows to a halt and I'm shaken from my stupor. I look around to see that we are in the drop-off line in front of my school.

"Want a hug before you get out?" Mom asks. I don't hesitate to accept and quickly wrap my arms around her. As I shut the passenger door behind me, I see her smiling just a little—a ghost of the smiles I used to see.

I can always tell her later.

In English, we're starting research papers. Supposedly, that will take us all the way to the end of the year. The senior class research paper never takes as long as the teachers expect, so the last real week of school ends up being a "watch movies in class or get your last-minute work turned in to your frazzled teacher" kind of week. This paper requires us to take at least two literary characters and compare them, using research from all these different academic databases to fully analyze them until we don't ever want to hear, speak, or read their names anymore for the rest of our lives.

I'm thinking of using Erik from the Phantom of the Opera. No idea who I could compare him to, but as long as I can BS my way through seven to ten pages, it should be an easy enough A once I get that figured out.

"Want me to grab you a Chromebook?" Val asks me, smiling as she stands, not waiting for my reply.

Val—Valentina Esparza—is and always has been the kind of person who never actually waits for your answer to that kind of question. A school project on a candy of our choosing brought us together in the seventh grade; we both picked Lemonheads, and we haven't looked back since. We've been practically inseparable since then.

"Thank you!" I half-shout to her back, since she's

already gone to get the Chromebooks so we can start looking up sources for our papers in the school's databases.

Once we've logged in, we begin our perfected ritual of pretending to be engrossed in our work while actually talking to one another with Chromebooks in front of us. It involves avoiding eye contact and pointing at each other's screens as if we're helping each other. If Mrs. McMyres is wise to our shenanigans, she gives us the dignity of pretending to be fooled by them.

"So, Tulip, how'd the talk with Tracy go?" Val asks me.

They say you're more likely to follow through with your plans if you share them with others. They are clearly wrong.

"Oh, uh, it was fine. I mean, she got upset, but—"

"Couldn't do it, huh?"

"Of course I couldn't; I looked at her, and it weakened my resolve."

9

Val *tsk, tsks* at me and shakes her head. Then she points to the Gmail icon at the bottom of my screen and says: "You've got to rip the band-aid off, chica."

"Maybe if I turn my back to her and then just spit it out all in one breath. Like, *MomI'msorrybutIwanttogoawayforcollegeandI'vealready beenaccepted!* Like that."

"That could work," Val nods, "Or maybe you could just grow the hell up and pause between words?" She nudges me playfully. She'll be going out of state for college on a tennis scholarship, an opportunity so good that even if Mr. and Mrs. Esparza did share my mom's clinginess, they'd still have no choice but to consent to her leaving because her older brother is still in college, and her twin brother will *also* be going to college next year.

"Hmm, interesting proposition." I tap my chin thoughtfully. "Or *maybe* my best friend in the whole wide world could tell her for me?" I look at her just long enough to wiggle my eyebrows at her enticingly before going back to facing my screen.

Val lets out an involuntary snort, "And break your poor mama's heart? Hell no!"

"Gee, thanks," I grumble before attempting to do something truly productive towards my essay. I know that it's abnormal for me to try and avoid hurting my mother as much as I do. I wish I could be more assertive, or at the very least passionate enough about anything to be more honest with her. In truth, I really don't know what I want to do beyond getting out of this town where I've spent my entire life, and that desire alone hardly seems like a good enough justification to make my mom as sad as I know my desire to leave will.

By the time the bell jolts me out of my deep thoughts, I've actually managed to find and save seven sources for my research paper—two more than the base requirement.

I take mine and Val's Chromebooks to the cart and we grab our bags to make our journey to the center of campus for lunch. We have a sizeable lunch group for two girls that fall somewhere on the low-to-middle end of the popularity spectrum. Most of the people in the group are more Val's friends than mine, but we all get along well.

By the time Val and I have reached our usual table, Laura and Reagan are already there holding hands and giggling to themselves. Val played a major part in setting them up, because—in her words— "they were both lonely lesbians, so *someone* had to intervene!" While I'm not 100% confident that her line of thinking on the subject isn't completely unproblematic, the two of them seem happier in the last three months of being a couple than either one of them had been separately for the entire time I've known them.

"You guys promised you wouldn't turn into one of those gross, cringey couples!" Val teases as we take our usual seats across from them and pull our lunches out of our bags.

"Oh, you're right. We should just be making out instead!" Laura fires back in her usual, more-hostile-than-necessary tone.

Val raises her hands to shield herself and turns her face away in horror, saying: "Please, by all means, continue to be cringey if that's the alternative."

I chuckle at the banter as our other two friends, Alondra and Stephanie arrive to their seats, lunch trays in hand.

Alondra addresses me: "Did you talk to your—"

Val cuts her off with a laugh: "You already know she didn't."

I sigh and nod in confirmation. I curse the idea that telling my friends my intentions would help keep me accountable.

"What a surprise, Tulip is still a coward." Laura scoffs without looking at me. Of all the people in my friend group, she is by far my least favorite, even though I've known her the longest.

"Sorry. I guess I didn't realize that not wanting to hurt your widowed mother's feelings was cowardly." I snap.

"The Dead Dad card is gonna expire before you know it." Laura retorts with an eye roll. I can never tell if her bitchiness is supposed to be playful or sincere, and I think that's what I dislike the most about her.

"Sheesh, babe," Reagan interjects, "can you, like, *chill?*"

I dig my peanut butter and jelly out from my brown bag and start tearing it apart, watching my pale fingers with much more focus than necessary so I don't cry in front of them. If I focus on sandwich ripping, I can't think about the sharp stabbing sensation Laura's words created behind my eyes.

"Your mom's probably freaked out by the idea of you leaving too far," Stephanie says helpfully, "I mean, you're the only kid they had, and with your dad gone…"

"Definitely," Alondra says, nodding, "I think it's totally normal for her to be a little clingy. It's probably been hard for her to adjust, right?"

I smile at them, grateful for their empathy where Laura has none.

"Yeah," I sigh, "but I also know I can't tether myself to her until *she's* comfortable letting me go."

"Right," Reagan agrees, "or you'll never be able

to live the life you dream of!"

Laura scoffs loudly, "Who says she can't live the life she dreams of if she goes to Edgecreek?" She cuts her eyes to me. "I'm going to Edgecreek next year, if you care to remember, and I'm excited about it. Are you too good to go to Edgecreek or something, Princess Tulip?"

I feel my mouth start to form into a snarl at her, and I make a conscious effort to stop it by wiping the back of my hand across my lips.

"It's not about that," I say defensively, "I just don't want to be stuck here forever. I want to live more than 40 minutes away from the town I was born in. Is that such a crime?"

After an awkward silence, Stephanie asks Laura and Reagan what she can expect in P.E. today, a distraction I am grateful for.

Val nudges me gently with her elbow and I give her a strained grin to signal that I'm fine before taking a bite of one of my sandwich fragments.

"I can't imagine how hard it is," Alondra murmurs so only I can hear from my other side. I turn my face towards her and see that she is looking at me earnestly. "You'll tell her when you're ready." She concludes with an air of finality.

The smile of gratitude I offer her in return is neither strained nor fake, but I do have to blink rather rapidly to keep my tears at bay.

"Here, you want my juice?" she asks, handing me the bulbous bottle off her tray, "I accidentally grabbed the wrong kind"

I take it and then immediately shake my head before placing it back on her lunch tray. "Thanks, but I can't. I'm allergic to pomegranates."

My last class of the day is Chemistry, and it's one of the few classes I don't share with Val. It's unfortunate, because the teacher, Coach Hart, doesn't like me. Like, at all. Val's presence would at least make the class somewhat bearable. In Coach Hart's defense, he's had to

16

deal with more than his fair share of conferences with my mother from the moment he handed back scores for our first test of the year. As much as I love my mom, even I can't deny that a parent-teacher conference with her is no walk in the park.

In my mom's defense, Coach Hart is a total bastard. His class, which I sense he is less than invested in, mostly involves him showing us episodes of CSI: Miami that he brings from home on DVD. He then tests on content from the textbooks we have never opened! Not surprisingly, I scored a D on Coach's Hart's first test of the year (my first failing grade *ever*). Of course, my mom scheduled a conference to ask him for guidance on how she could help me do better on the next test.

I wasn't there for this conversation, but was told several times, with increasing amounts of animation from my mom with each retelling, that he shrugged at her and said: "I dunno… She could study?" Their relationship hasn't exactly been amicable since then. On the plus side, once he realized that the only way to keep Tracy Burns off his back was to pass me, he started giving me Cs on all my tests without even looking at them. I guess he didn't want the drama with my mom to affect his baseball season, not that I'd ever complain about that.

I stroll to my seat in the back of the room and, as always, I'm the first to arrive. While Val isn't in this class to suffer with me, Stephanie is. She's usually barely on time because she spends passing period sucking face with her boyfriend Levi in the hall. That is, when they aren't having weepy arguments about what next year will mean for their relationship.

For as long as I've known Stephanie, she has always tended to jump into relationships with very passionate boys who like her *way* more than she could ever like them. She dates to have fun and be adored, verging on obsession; when the guy switches from hot to annoying, she trades up fast. A part of me begrudgingly respects that about her, but I hate how she can hurt the boys who would do just about anything for her.

Of all my friends, Stephanie is the one with the most dating experience, hands down. Laura and Reagan probably came in second, since they were both each other's second relationship—Laura, who has known she was a lesbian since kindergarten, had never wasted her time trying to have boyfriends; meanwhile, Reagan had one boyfriend during freshman year, which is when she started questioning her sexuality. That boyfriend told her she would go to Hell for what she discovered about herself. She broke up with him and started dating a Ukrainian exchange student named Anya. Both Reagan and Laura spent their sophomore and junior years single, and it drove Val crazy enough to intervene *this* year and set them up.

Alondra and I are on the same level in terms of romantic history; we each had one boyfriend during freshman year. But while Alondra is the most boy-crazy person I've ever met, and turns into a blushing, eyelash-fluttering mess when a good-looking guy gives her attention, I tend to develop feelings for people slowly, after I actually get to know them, regardless of gender.

As for Val, I know she likes guys and has even

had crushes on a handful of them. She's just never dated anyone and often tells me that it's a waste of time to date in high school anyway. At least it is for *her*.

I'm watching the door to avoid looking in Coach Hart's direction, when Tony Jackson, my other friend in this class, walks in. We have been friends since first grade, and no matter how long it's been since we've seen each other, as soon as we are within an arm's reach, we slip right back into comfortable familiarity.

Tony locks eyes with me and returns my smile as he bounces towards his seat, right behind mine. The only difference between our smiles is that mine is utterly goofy—some might even say awkward and clownish when paired with my orange hair and clam-white skin. Tony's smile, on the other hand, is both gorgeous and full of mischief. Tony is cute and knows it, with his warm russet brown skin, agate-green eyes, and head full of tight, dark curls. His smile and natural charm have, for as long as I've known him, gotten him out of trouble countless times, and into the daydreams and fantasies of countless girls. Alondra has been his number one fan for two years and counting.

"Lovely as always, Babygirl," Tony says, squeezing my shoulder as he moves past me to get to his desk.

I roll my eyes and shake my head as I turn in my seat to face him. "Steph out there?" I ask.

His turn to roll his eyes. "Yeah, being *nasty* with her boy-toy." He pulls a pack of gum out of his pocket and slides into a lounging position in his hard plastic desk chair as he offers me the pack first.

I gasp in exaggerated delight and say: "You take such good care of me!" in a thick, southern drawl.

Tony smacks his lips and replies: "Well, someone's got to. You're useless."

I playfully swat at him and miss, eliciting a chuckle from us both. In all honesty, while Tony has always been kind to me, he has treated me with extra tenderness since my dad died, always looking out for me and having my back, even at the funeral.

Well, especially at the funeral. I had been

hovering near the wall, not wanting to look towards my dad's casket, not talking to anyone, when Tony approached me. I remember looking into those gemstone eyes of his and seeing no trace of humor in them for the first time ever, and when he wordlessly hugged me, a dam inside me finally broke and I sobbed into his chest until my throat hurt and my hands cramped from squeezing them into fists near my face as he just held me and rubbed my back.

Neither of us said anything, but he handed me a tissue he'd had tucked into the sleeve of his shirt when I straightened up, then brushed a soft kiss against my forehead and walked to his seat just as Val and my other friends arrived. For the rest of the funeral and reception, anytime I'd look around I would find him nearby, watching me in case I needed him.

That's kind of how he's been with me ever since.

Right as the bell rings, Stephanie rushes in and plops down into the desk next to mine, her face and chest flushed. Coach Hart says nothing as he walks to shut the door and flick off the lights, smacking his gum loudly.

22

Projected onto the whiteboard at the front of the class is the paused opening credits to *CSI: Miami*.

Coach Hart drags his feet to his desk and hits play, allowing Roger Daltrey's scream to signal that class has started.

CHAPTER TWO

I walk through the door of my empty house after having waved goodbye to Val. Mom texted me as my classmates and I watched Horatio Caine solve yet another crime to let me know that she'd gotten hung up at work and wouldn't be able to get me from school. Val giddily accepted the once-rare opportunity to drive me, since it always used to be a red-letter day on the calendar when my mom lets anyone else drive me anywhere.

That was before everything in our lives changed, of course.

In her text, my mom had also given me the green light to have pizza delivered and requested that I go check in on the plants and give them a little bit of my magic touch.

Before he got sick, my dad built a greenhouse in the backyard. It's nothing fancy, just one of those tiny little huts that come in a build-it-yourself kit with the Amazon smile on the box, but at the time, it was absolutely perfect for Mom's short-lived obsession with growing her own tomatoes, and my love of all things that grow from dirt. Once Mom discovered that she couldn't keep a single tomato plant alive to save her life, it turned into the place where she puts all the succulents that she can't stop herself from buying from the floral department of any grocery store, and where I tend to any plants I can find that need a little help staying alive.

I quickly order pizza on the app on my phone—light sauce, stuffed crust, extra-extra cheese—and head out the back door to take care of my plant babies.

Our yard has no fence and backs up to a large,

grassy field that has managed to remain undeveloped by some miracle. I look out across it now and see a slight breeze turning the grass into a calm ocean. I smile, completely at ease, and go into the greenhouse.

Entering this space always sends a wave of peace and joy through me. It's like a quiet hum that vibrates my body from the inside as I walk in and survey the plants.

I see that, despite the impossibility of it, my mother has indeed managed to do something to one of her moonstone succulents to cause it to yellow slightly and start to wrinkle on the edges.

Too much water, I hear my internal voice whisper.

I get to work on removing the poor thing from its little pot to check the roots. I examine the plant and clearly cut all the roots that are hurting it, then give it a bed of nice, fresh soil in its pot, which I then gently tuck it into. Looking down at it as I put it back in its place on the shelf, I sense a feeling of what I can only describe as gratitude radiating off it. That, and simple relief, like the first breath taken after trying for too long to touch the bottom of the deep end in the pool.

Satisfied, I turn my attention to the Boston Fern I've been tending to for a week or so. One of our neighbors had placed it by the street on trash day—I can only assume because they thought it was done-for, given that half its leaves were yellow and brittle. I ran over just in time to snatch it up before the trash guys did, and I've been rehabilitating it ever since.

It's already much perkier than it was, and it looks like it will make a full recovery. I grab the spray bottle next to it and spritz its leaves until they are nice and dewy. For just a moment it looks like the fronds are all reaching up towards me like a small child asking for a hug, so I lean closer and gently nuzzle the plant, feeling my little green child's arms embrace me.

My phone vibrates to let me know the pizza will be here soon, so I reluctantly leave the greenhouse, hovering my hands over any plant I pass by as a silent farewell.

I feel a peace that I rarely experience since my

dad died. Something about being in our greenhouse, or even just in nature puts me at ease, and I yearn for it like a drug most days. I don't mind things like school that require me to be inside, because I know they're a necessary part of life, but if it were up to me, I would spend all day, every day outdoors among plants, or under a canopy of trees.

Wanting just one more fix before heading back inside, I look over my shoulder to cast a glance at the grass field.

This time, when I look across it, I feel my stomach drop.

I sense her presence before I really see her, but she doesn't take long to spot. She's tall, I can tell as much even from the great distance between us. She's clear across the grass field from me, almost like she emerged from the small, wooded area beyond it—a minuscule "woods" full of cedar trees and dead cottonwoods that's polluted with snakes and sickly deer. She's thin too, like a runway model with dark, almost black hair that caresses her bare shoulders. And she's dressed in a black camisole top with black pants, and she's staring at me.

She's too far away for me to be able to make out her expression, but she is motionless as a statue, and there is no mistaking the fact that her face is pointed in my direction.

I freeze at the realization. I stare back, eyes wide. I feel the skin of my face tingle as it is drained of color. All the peace I had felt just seconds ago evaporates as I stare at this person with pale skin, dark clothes and even darker hair, who is staring back at me.

And in the back—the *very* back—of my mind is the faintest tickle of recognition. Though there is 99% of me that is absolutely sure I've never met her before, that tickle back there, *just* out of my reach, keeps insisting that I *know* her.

Apprehensive and eager to shed this unease like a coat that's too warm to wear, I force myself to turn back towards my house and make my way inside.

I don't turn back until I am closing the sliding

glass door behind me, which is impressive, because I was sure I would hear the thumping sound of what would have been her tastefully worn-down Dr. Martens racing toward my turned back the entire time I walked to my house. But now that I have all the security that a double pane of glass can provide between us, I look to see if she's still there.

Gone.

I look around the outer edge of the field and even do a quick scan of my own backyard, but she's gone. It's as though she was never there to begin with.

I rake my eyes across the tree line she had been standing in front of and still see no trace of her. My eyes linger for a moment at the spot where she stood and it's almost as though I can still feel her there.

With a shiver, I slide the door closed and lock it. I take only one step away before deciding to draw the blackout curtains in front of it closed, for good measure.

While I wait for my pizza to arrive, all I can think is: *This is fine. Not scary at all.*

Mom gets home before the pizza even has time to get cold. She's wearing her unicorn scrubs (which I think more medical professionals should wear, not just the ones in pediatrics like her). I'm working on my third slice of cheesy deliciousness when she walks into the kitchen.

"Hi," I say, "thanks for letting Val drive me home today. She was super excited about it."

"Thank *her* for me next time you talk to her, would you?" She says in a winded tone, slipping off her Crocs. "Did you order the usual?"

"Yep! Want some?"

"No, take it for lunch tomorrow. I'm not very hungry." She walks over and sits down across the table from me, resting her head on her hands, eyes closed. I take a silent inventory of her appearance:

No makeup. Not even Mascara.

Red nose, probably from crying in the car on her way home.

Deep purple bags under her eyes.

Hair in a low ponytail that's fairly neat, except for some flyaway hairs up top.

She hasn't been the same since Dad died, and at this point I'm not sure if she's *ever* going to recover. Even when he was first diagnosed, she was still the picture of optimism. *We will fight, we can beat this, 98% survival rate* and all that other stuff. Then, it turned out to be worse than anyone initially believed. Then, he started having heart problems on top of the cancer. Then, despite all the optimism and can-do spirit Mom was putting out into the universe on Dad's behalf, we found out that all that fighting and hope didn't actually help him beat it, and it was like a part of her died too and was laid to rest in the casket with him.

I considered, when she walked in, telling her about the girl across the field. Looking at her now, though, I decide against it. It's not like anything can be done about her now, except keep my eyes peeled for her, anyway.

I also consider opening up the dialogue about my

college plans, but I can't bring myself to broach that topic either.

Maybe I'll go to whatever college I pick and not tell her until moving day.

Mom rubs her eyes lazily, then gazes across the table at me. Her brow furrows after a second of taking in my face.

"You okay?" she asks in a voice both weary and concerned.

"Yeah!" I say, *way* cheerier than I had meant to. "All good here!"

Mom goes to bed not long after that, leaving me to my own devices on the condition that I don't get crazy or stay up too late, considering it's only Thursday.

I plop down on the couch after turning all the lights off, and turn on Jennifer's Body. Horror movies before bed help me sleep better. Dad used to joke that it was proof of some level of craziness in me.

I pull out my phone and text Val: *Guess who has full reign of the living room!!!*

A moment later, Val responds: *Heck yeah!!! Horror movies all night??*

I reply: *You know it! Dude, my mom looked rough. I feel like it's never gonna be a good time to talk to her. :(*

Val is a lot slower to respond this time, but when she does, her text says: *You may be right. Buuuuuuut, that doesn't mean you shouldn't talk to her. She's got to know before she sends your room and board deposit. It's going to suck, but what are you gonna do, just go to a school you don't want to go to and be miserable?*

I begin typing out a simple *You're right, I know it,* but I don't send it. We've had this conversation so many times already, and I'm sure she's getting fed up with having to give me the same advice. I know she's right. I also know that Laura is right, in her own way, I am a coward.

It isn't just that I'm afraid of hurting my mom. It isn't *just* that I don't want to make her feel abandoned. It's *also* that I'm terrified of disappointing her by not living up to the person she's built me up as in her head.

The Tulip that exists in her mind is driven and level-headed, and wants to be a dentist because it's a good, solid job. The Tulip out here in the real world gets by on luck and the help of her friends. She doesn't know with 100% certainty what she wants to do with her life, but she knows that she loves writing poetry, singing, and plants. She knows with 100% certainty that she wants to be happy when she grows up. And while that might make a lovely John Lennon quote, it doesn't offer much in the way of the kind of stability that every parent like my mom hopes for, for their child.

Mom's Tulip is perfect, but *I* am far from it.

Just as Jennifer tears out a boy's throat, I get a text from Tony. It's just a blurry, dark image of what looks like his front yard, cars parked in the driveway with the dusky sky in the background. But then I see a shadowy figure in the distance, beyond the cars in his driveway. I feel a chill run up my back. I had managed to forget about earlier with the girl in black, but suddenly I feel punched in the face by the memory.

I text back: *Lol, are we communicating in only*

pictures now?

I watch the three dots appear, indicating that Tony's replying, feeling suddenly uneasy.

When he finally sends his response, I feel my throat tighten.

He says: *Someone's standing outside watching me!*

CHAPTER THREE

I tried calling Tony as soon as I read his text last night. I tried three times, only to be sent to voicemail. He never called me back, but he did send a text that said: *talking to a cop*. I had replied, only asking him to keep me updated, but I hadn't heard from him again.

So, now I sit outside the weight room at school, after having made Mom drop me off early, and wait for the boys' track team to finish whatever training they do in there so I can talk to him.

I haven't been able to shake the unease I felt

upon first reading his text. It could be completely unrelated to the girl I saw yesterday, but somehow, I doubt that.

At exactly seven minutes before the first bell, the guys start filing out of the gym and into the locker room next to me. I catch a few of them looking me up and down and it sends a searing flush across my cheeks. It doesn't escape my notice that several of them have their shirts off and are glistening with sweat under the fluorescents.

I push my hair behind my ears to give my hands something to do, suddenly uncomfortably aware of my every move.

Tony and I lock eyes the moment he steps out of the gym. He grins at me and I step to the side, tilting my head in the direction of my movement. He follows suit.

I lean against the wall behind me and look at him. He's almost a foot taller than I am, and if I were to look straight in front of me, I'd be making perfect eye contact with his nipples, which I might not have known if they weren't currently staring me down from their spots on his bare, sweaty chest, burning holes into me with their gaze.

"My eyes are up here, you perv," Tony says, chuckling.

"Sorry," I clear my throat, shake my head, and peel my eyes away from his *very* chiseled chest to look him in the eyes. "You never told me what happened last night. I was worried!"

He shrugs. "There wasn't really much to tell. By the time the cop got to the house, the guy was gone. So, then the cop was acting like we were just wasting his time. Like, yeah, we just wanted you to come over and hang. Okay, bro."

"A guy?" I ask, louder than I intended. I lower my voice and continue: "It was a guy outside your house? Not a girl?"

He arches an eyebrow at me. "That's a weird question."

"Well—" I sigh. Do I tell him about the girl? What good would it do? Probably none. But I look into

Tony's eyes—Tony, who I've known since first grade, whose every birthday party since that year I've been to, who let me soak his shirt with my tears at my dad's funeral, and I know I can't lie to him or pretend it was just a random question.

His brow furrows in confusion at my silence.

"I saw a girl yesterday, dressed in all black who wa... who *seemed* to be watching me at my house."

Tony crosses his arms and widens his stance, looking down at me now with concern and confusion painted across his face in equal measure. "Who was it?" he asks.

"I don't know. You know that field behind us that goes to the woods?"

He nods.

"Well, she was standing on the other side of that field. I went out to the greenhouse and she wasn't there, but when I came out, she was. And by the time I made it back to the house, she was gone again."

Tony's mouth is turned downward, and he nods

slowly, pensively, still burning into my soul with his eyes.

"So," I continue, "when you texted that someone was outside *your* house, I thought maybe it was her. I thought… Well, hell, I don't know what I thought." I raise my hands to shoulder height and let them drop as a show of my exasperation.

Tony is still nodding. He inhales deeply and slowly through his nose. His face loosens. He shakes his head and shifts his weight to one foot. He seems as dumbfounded as I feel.

"I guess it's stupid," I say. "Saying it out loud, it's stupid."

He *tsks* at me once and says, "It's not stupid. It's definitely weird. Hard to think it could be a coincidence." He looks at me again and shrugs.

I shrug too. "Nothing, I guess." I pick myself up off the wall behind me. "Anyway, sorry for holding you up." I loosen the hair from behind my ears as I look down at my feet, suddenly embarrassed that I'd waited for him outside of practice.

Tony says nothing.

I look back up at him. His stance hasn't changed, but now he's looking down at me with an odd but intense expression. His brow is furrowed again and his lips are slightly parted. His eyes have become glassy and absent. They look searching and almost sad.

My brow furrows, mirroring his. "Um," I say, blushing, "you okay?"

"Yeah…" he replies, slowly. "Sorry, weird Déjà vu moment. I haven't slept well for a couple of nights. Weird dreams. Guess it's getting to me." His voice is monotone; each sentence is a staccato.

"Okay…" I say.

Without warning, and very quickly, he raises one of his arms towards me, bringing his hand so close to my face that I can feel his body heat radiating off of him. Before I can ask what he's doing, his index finger brushes ever so slightly against my cheekbone before it twirls a loose lock of my hair around. His gaze shifts from me, to that lock of my hair around his finger.

Deep within the lowest part of my belly, I feel a fluttering and a rush of pleasant warmth. My back straightens, and I gasp slightly at his touch.

After a moment, I clear my throat and say, "Well, you'd better go get dressed. I'll see you in Chemistry?"

"Yeah," he says, blinking rapidly and dropping his hand with a slight shake of his head, "Yeah, see you later."

We part ways quickly, with him going towards the locker room, while I go in the other direction, barely even registering that this wasn't the way to my first period class.

What was that?

All day long, the ghost of Tony's touch has haunted my cheekbone. I've been hyper-aware of the spot where his skin touched mine in every class and at lunch. Even the roots of the individual hairs that he touched have been feeling like they're vibrating with

43

electricity.

In all the years we've known each other, the adults in our lives have often joked with our parents that we were going to get married one day. One of those weird fantasies that some people, who can't wrap their minds around a boy and a girl being close friends, like to build in their own minds, I guess. But for our part, Tony and I have never dated, or even acted out a playground romance.

That's not to say that I've never thought about it. I've certainly had one or two crushes on him over the years, especially when, in sixth grade, his voice dropped earlier than any of the other boys I'd known then. Or when, in ninth grade, the last of his baby fat had melted away, and playing football had caused his body to harden into the smooth curves of defined muscles and make his whole back turn into a V-shape. And then of course last year, when he treated me with such kindness and tenderness at the funeral, it was hard to convince myself, as I had every other time, that crushes destroy friendships. Even friendships as special as ours.

Also, I've never deluded myself into thinking I was Tony's type.

Tony is and always has been all charisma. One smile of his can get him both into and out of trouble in seconds. Everyone who knows him adores him. He's athletic, he's popular, and he's gorgeous. I, on the other hand, tend to fly under the social radar; I am as far from an athlete as a person can get, am awkward enough that my life should have a soundtrack of exclusively tuba and bass music, and have always preferred plants to people.

That's not to say that I think there's anything inherently wrong with any of that; on the contrary, I actually love the way I am when I avoid thinking about the fact that I can't make myself talk to my mom about college. But, I know that my style is not for everyone, and it would be stupid to pretend that someone like Tony would ever see me as more than a friend.

Still, as I sit at my desk in Chemistry, I can't seem to peel my eyes away from the door, or still the butterflies that have made their home in my stomach.

When Steph enters the room, her eyes are puffy

since today is apparently a fight day. Disappointingly, I think that Tony must have gone home early.

Why should I care? I think, shaking my head at myself.

The bell rings and Coach Hart drags his feet towards the door to close it when Tony appears in the door frame.

"Get to class on time, Jackson." He barks with barely disguised apathy.

"Sorry, Coach." I hear Tony mutter before stepping around Coach Hart. His eyes dart to mine almost instantly before we both look away.

Stephanie looks over her shoulder at me with a cheeky grin. Even on days when she's in the throes of her own personal soap opera, she can't resist an opportunity to tease me about boys.

I feel heat spread across my cheeks as Tony takes his seat behind me.

Coach Hart stands at the front of the room to address us. His head is tilted back, and he seems to be talking to a spot on the back wall more than to us when he says, "We're doing a lab today. Partner up. Come get the supplies off my desk. Find a lab table and get to it." He slumps back behind his desk, where several small boxes are piled up, and flops into his seat. He's probably worn out from the effort of talking to us for so long.

Steph turns in her seat and places her hand on mine where it rests on top of my desk. "Partners?" she asks.

I nod, and we rise from our seats to get the materials and then find an empty lab table in the back of the room. I feel a slight pang of disappointment at not having gotten to ask Tony to be partners, but given how my heart pounded at just having him sit behind me in his usual desk, it's probably for the best.

The table Steph and I claimed is right in the middle of the back row of lab tables. As we unpack our supplies, I glance up and see Tony walking with a guy in our class named Jesse. I think they know each other from football.

Tony's eyes lock with mine as he and Jesse walk

past Steph and me at our table. His usual mischievous glimmer is gone, replaced with something I can't quite put my finger on—something *intense* that is causing heat to fill my insides and the air I breathe to feel thick as he holds onto my gaze.

I force myself not to turn my head to keep watching him as they pass. I am practically panting as Steph and I look at our spread-out supplies.

Two beakers, a square of aluminum foil, a metal stick, a funnel, a little baggie of tiny green crystals, and a ring stand.

We look up at Coach Hart expectantly. He is staring at his phone, looking incredibly bored.

One of the girls at the front lab table, a rather mousy try-hard named Caroline, raises her hand.

Coach Hart is still staring at his phone.

Caroline clears her throat uncomfortably.

Coach Hart's only movement is to raise one eyebrow and roll his eyes in Caroline's direction.

"Um, Coach? What should we do now?" Caroline squeaks.

Coach Hart lets out an exasperated sigh, and with yet another roll of his eyes, says: "Follow the instructions in the packet."

"Prick," Steph mumbles so only I can hear her.

I pick up the packet that had been at the bottom of our supplies box and hold it up so both of us can read it. The ocean wave sound from sliding papers around me indicates that everyone else is doing the same thing.

"Green Chunks and Foil." Steph reads the title aloud.

"Charming," I reply.

We read the instructions all the way through twice before either of us can comprehend them. The whole time, I feel the heat of someone staring at my back. I don't even have to look around to know that it's Tony. I think I could even accurately guess where exactly he is behind me. It's like I can *sense* him through an invisible cord tying us together.

Steph takes the lead on this joke of a lab because she can tell I'm distracted. She reads every step of the instructions aloud to me while I use our materials to complete each one.

When I accidentally grab the filter paper instead of the funnel, Steph snickers at me but reaches her hand over me to do this step herself.

I can't help it. I look over my shoulder, but I toss my hair to maybe give the impression that it's just in my way.

Tony is three tables behind me, and sure enough we lock eyes at the same time. His forehead is wrinkled with the furrow of his brow line and glistens with a tiny layer of sweat now. My breath catches in my chest at the collision of our eyes and the pressure in my stomach intensifies.

Are they butterflies or bats I feel in there?

I turn back to face my own table so quickly that my hair whips Steph on her shoulder. I feel my chest practically heaving now, as though I've run a mile.

"Dude, what are you doing?!" A male voice cries out from behind me.

Followed immediately by the shattering of glass.

Steph and I—and everyone around us—jump at the startling sound, turning to find the source.

The voice, as it turns out, was Jesse.

The glass, as it turns out, had been the beaker in Tony's hand. Now it is in shards that are scattered on the table in front of him on the floor and embedded in his hand. Blood is already starting to drip from his palm, down his fingers, and onto the table.

I look in horror at the bloody mess for only a second before my eyes shift to Tony's face which is now contorted in shock.

Tony's full lips are parted slightly. His green eyes are as big as plates, and now there are thick tears, like melting wax on a candlestick, flowing from them. And they are fixed on me so pointedly that even our classmates keep looking back and forth between us almost uncomfortably.

I gape at him, full of concern and something else too… That same *tickle* at the back of my mind.

Even Coach Hart has been startled out of his seat. "Go to the nurse, Jackson!" He commands as he makes his way across the room towards us with a broom he got from somewhere behind his desk.

Tony jumps at Coach Hart's voice, looks around as if finally realizing where he is, and nods wordlessly but almost immediately looks back at me for what feels like a full minute before he actually starts moving towards the door to leave.

He passes by me on his way out, maintaining eye contact until he's past, with tears still rolling down his cheeks. I watch as one drop reaches the edge of his jaw and pauses just briefly before it plops hard and heavy on the corner of the table.

In the shocked silence of this room, the sound of it is as loud as the crash of thunder.

CHAPTER FOUR

Tony never came back to class. Not even to get his backpack. After the bell rang for dismissal, I even went by the nurse's office only to find it empty. Now I stand outside of the school's main entrance, knowing logically that I'm supposed to be looking for my mom's car, but feeling on a deep and emotional level that I'm lost.

A car horn startles me out of the fog I'm in. I look around and see Mom waving at me from her spot in the pick-up line. I wave back weakly and walk toward the car.

As I make my way to the car so I can start my weekend and distance myself from this weirdness, I absentmindedly cast a glance around at all the other cars. That's when I notice, over by the entrance to the parking lot, *her* leaning up against the school's marquee.

The girl from last night is standing there, leaning against the marquee with one foot propped up behind her. She's dressed in all black again, though this time she isn't staring at me. At least, not outright. Her gaze drifts back and forth between me as I slow my walk to the car, and the two guys standing in front of her. One of them, I don't recognize. He, like her, has a head full of jet-black hair and wears all dark colors—black jeans, a gray shirt, and black combat boots.

The other guy is Tony. My stomach tightens uncomfortably, and my mouth suddenly feels dry. His hand is freshly bandaged, and I see him speaking urgently and animatedly to her as she continues to shift her face and focus between him and me.

That *tickle* again. This time, it is stronger than ever. Strong enough that I find myself absentmindedly scratching the back of my head.

I don't realize that I'm standing still and staring at the three of them until I hear another car horn. I whip my head around to see my mom once again waving frantically from the driver's seat, trying to hurry me along.

I snap back to attention and hurry towards the car, if only to force the day to be over. I don't look towards the marquee again as I make my way to the car, though I feel nearly certain that they're all looking at me now.

"Who were you staring those daggers at?" Mom asks as I throw myself into the passenger's seat.

"I wasn't staring daggers," I say, pulling the car door shut behind me.

Mom cranes her neck to look in the direction of the marquee. "Oh, it's Tony!" she says with a noticeable warmth in her tone. "Who's that he's with?"

I look back over at them. Tony's face is downturned now, and the girl is talking to him while the guy nods along.

"I wish I knew," I mutter.

Most Friday nights, I sleep over at Val's house. Tonight is a rare exception because her dad has to get up early tomorrow and we tend to keep him awake with the shenanigans of our youth. So instead, we are on FaceTime while we both watch Sleepaway Camp.

"Oh my *gawd*!" Val laughs through my phone screen. "Angela is giving her the murder eyes!"

I cackle in response and say: "She's like, 'sure, I'll go swimming… In your blood!'"

It is well past midnight. I sit on the couch in the living room and have to speak to Val primarily in whispers so I don't wake Mom up.

"Girl!" Val says, "Speaking of blood, what happened in Chem?!"

I sigh. "No idea. Tony was acting weird. Did you talk to him?"

Val *tsks* and replies: "No. I tried, but it was like he had blinders on. Just zoomed right by me. I was going to the bathroom, and he walked past me, I guess towards the nurse's office. He was bleeding a ton!"

"Yeah, somehow he broke his beaker." I reach for the remote, suddenly not quite as invested in the movie.

Val snickers as I turn the TV off and make my way to my bedroom at the front of the house. "Sounds like a sad euphemism or something." She says.

I give a halfhearted chuckle as I flip on my light switch. My bedroom looks small, but only because of all the clutter scattered around and all the posters taped to every wall in diagonal, overlapping patterns. The clutter consists mostly of stuffed animals and stacks of books and craft projects, both of which are almost always left unfinished. Mom says she can't come into my room because it stresses her out with its lack of order, but I know the general locations of everything when I need it.

Val notices my sudden change of scenery. "Hey!" she says, "No more movie?"

"Eh," I say, suddenly sadder than I want to admit. "I'm not really feeling it so much anymore."

"Why, what's wrong?" Val asks, pausing the movie on her end.

"Honestly? I don't even know. I've been feeling weird all day. Tony and I had... Like, a *moment* this morning, and I guess I just can't shake it off. It's stupid."

"What do you mean by *moment*?"

"Well," I sigh and flop down onto my bed, "he, like... Stroked my hair and touched my cheek."

Val waits for a beat, then says: "That's it?"

"Well, yeah," I say, not understanding how that doesn't strike her as weird.

"That doesn't sound all that *moment*-y to me. You two have always been, like, weirdly affectionate with each other."

"I don't know," I say, more defensive than I care to admit, and a little embarrassed at having said anything at all, "it just felt different, and I can't explain it."

Val laughs. I blush. Outside my window, I hear the light tap of a lightning bug, and it's probably laughing at me too.

"Well," Val sighs, "Maybe you just *like* him and it's as simple as that?"

I open my mouth to respond when I hear another tap on my window. This time, it's much more pronounced and intentional. My heart feels like it has frozen suddenly. I look toward my window and hold my breath.

Tap, tap, tap.

"Hey, Val, can I call you tomorrow? I heard something…"

"Wait, seriously?! Wh—"

I end the call, cutting her off.

Tap, tap, tap. A little harder, more urgent.

I rise to my feet and approach the window. I reach a shaking hand out in front of me to push aside my blackout curtain. My heart pounds in my ears like a bass drum, increasing in tempo. My breathing is shallow and rapid. But, I feel an undeniable need to see what's on the other side of the curtain.

I push the curtain aside and slowly raise one of the blinds.

All I see is the black of night.

I take a deep, steadying breath and inch my face closer to the gap I've created between the blinds and peek out into the dark.

My eyes struggle to cling to any discernible shape as they adjust to the darkness. Within a few seconds, I'm able to make out the outline of Mom's car in the driveway to my left. I glide my eyes slowly to the right and scan my front yard.

Suddenly, my eyes connect with a pair of jade-green ones. I gasp and jump back as my heart threatens to break through my ribcage.

Then, realization hits; I know those eyes.

I open the curtain fully and raise the blinds, followed by the window so that it's only the mesh screen separating Tony and me.

"What are you doing here?!" I hiss at him.

Tony leans forward to bring himself to my eye level. His face is inches away from mine. His hands are placed on the outside ledge of my window to prop him up, and the stark white bandage around the one practically glows in the moonlight.

He doesn't say anything, just stares at me. His eyes are searching my face with an intensity that I'm not used to from anyone. Despite myself, I feel blood warming my cheeks and a couple of other places.

Embarrassed by my own biology, I clear my throat and mumble: "I've been really worried about you."

"I can't believe it," Tony breathes, "I can't believe I never realized…" He trails off, shaking his head, still looking at my face with an expression that is making me ache to reach out and touch him.

As if of its own free will, my hand goes to the screen and rests there, my palm facing Tony, my fingers spread.

He sighs and places his hand up on the screen to meet mine. His heat radiates into my palm, making me hyper-aware of my own pulse there.

I can't help remembering the old Romeo and Juliet movie from the sixties that we watched in Freshman English. How we, as a class, cringed at the two actors in that scene where Romeo and Juliet first meet. I feel like if anyone could see us like this—Tony and I—we'd get laughed at just as harshly.

But there's also something about even just the small touch we're doing that feels like the sudden release of tension. It's like I had an itch I couldn't reach, and I finally got it scratched. So, as laughable and random and sudden and crazy as it is, I let myself feel the relief his touch is giving me.

I drag my eyes from our hands back to Tony's face and, for what feels simultaneously like seconds and hours, we stand there drinking each other in. All the things I needed to know earlier about who the girl in black was, how Tony knows her and the guy she was with, seem less important now. They can be Future Tulip's problem.

Then Tony stands fully and breaks the connection of our hands.

"I can't stay," he murmurs. "I just needed to see you. I know I should have waited until…" he trails off.

"Until when?" I ask.

Tony sighs and shakes his head. "I just needed to see you." He repeats. Then, he begins backing away to leave, like he's not quite ready to stop looking at me yet. He walks backward for three or four steps before he turns and jogs toward the end of my street where, I assume, he parked his car.

I watch until I can no longer see him. And then I keep watching, just to make sure I can't see him. When I turn back to face the rest of my bedroom, the glow of my light seems warmer than usual, and my head feels drunk from the encounter. I find myself wishing he would come back, my stomach twisting with anxiety now that he's gone.

Does he like me? I wonder. *Is that what he meant?*

I can't even begin to decipher the things that Tony said—I can hardly even remember them with the way my head is swimming right now.

I *want* Tony to like me. This morning, I woke up and he was *just* Tony, one of my oldest friends. But something has undeniably shifted, and it seems much deeper and more permanent than any of the times in the past that I've *liked* him. It's like he's pulling me towards him, like a magnet... Like even if I tried to resist, I still wouldn't be able to break the force of his pull.

But I don't *want* to break it.

CHAPTER FIVE

Water dripping.

The smell of sulfur.

A field of wildflowers. Poppies.

A flash of color in front of my eyes. Color and light. Then, darkness. Black eyes.

The mournful sound of weeping. Somewhere. Echoing.

A fire in a torch.

A man's face. *Father*.

An arm, thick, strong, smooth, wrapped around my waist. I am pulled, backwards and downwards.

A dog's snores, deep and rumbling.

A river flows.

A mirror, large and silver and shining at the end of a long, dark hallway.

I float towards it, gliding through the air, and it grows larger and larger, and my body moves faster and faster and I am hurtling towards it. I see a shape, dark and unfocused, taking form in it and I stare at it, breathing, and I strain my eyes to make out one distinguishable feature in this form in this mirror in this dark hallway coated with shadow, cries echoing all around me.

Awaken!

I sit up in my bed, gasping for air.

Sunlight leaks into the room from the spaces between my blinds and curtains. On the nightstand beside me, my phone vibrates. I turn to look at it and see that I have five texts from Val *and* that it's 11 AM.

Rubbing my eyes with one hand, I grab my phone with the other to see Val's texts. All of them are essentially the same: *Girl, text me so I know you aren't murdered!* Though she did use varying degrees of capitalization and exclamation in each one.

I text her: *Sorry, just woke up. Everything's fine!* And then I throw myself backward onto the bed. My head is throbbing and the sweat coating my body has already turned cold. My heart is racing but I feel the edge of panic already beginning to dull.

What did I dream about? I wonder. Already the memory of the dream is fading.

I should get up. Mom might worry if I stay in bed any longer, so I should *definitely* get up. I *want* to get up, or at least I will want to get up if I keep telling myself that I do. My body feels heavy; my limbs are four sacks full of lead and sand and Jell-O.

This feels a little like what I remember my last flu feeling like. The throbbing in my head is like a relentless drum pounding and pounding.

I feel my phone vibrate under my palm, turned face down on my belly, and I don't even have the willpower to check it. It's probably just Val texting me back anyway.

I suddenly realize how quiet the rest of the house is, and that's enough to roll my heavy body off the bed. Mom has never been a morning person exactly, but she still can't ever seem to sleep past 8:30 on a weekend. Normally, the smell of biscuits from a can heating up in the oven would have crawled through the air to my room to wake me, but today there is nothing.

I sluggishly lift myself from my cocoon by first throwing my feet to the floor, letting the inertia pull the rest of my body into a sitting position. I stretch my arms up and out into a Y-shape, trying to force the flow of blood to my extremities with a long stretch. When that's done, I leave my room in search of signs of life.

My feet bare, I pad down the hall towards the living room and kitchen. The only sound is the gentle roar of the AC. I find both rooms— which used to overflow with warmth and activity on the weekends—cold, silent, and sad. I can't think of a single time in my entire life when a Saturday morning wasn't marked by freshly baked biscuits waiting for me on a serving tray on the kitchen counter, and my parents busying themselves with weekend projects.

Even after Dad died, Mom still *always* got up and made biscuits on Saturday mornings without fail. They'd stay on the serving tray for us to pick from all morning, and when lunchtime came around, they'd be thrown in sandwich bags and put in the refrigerator for later. Seeing no activity when I wake up is something I've gotten used to, but to wake up and find no biscuits? It's unsettling.

Brow furrowed, I quietly make my way towards' my parents' room on the other side of the house. I've tried to avoid their room as much as I could since the day of Dad's funeral.

I had sat at the foot of their bed, already dressed in a navy-blue blouse that was too tight around my armpits and a pair of black slacks that were too tight around my waist yet too loose around my ankles. I felt like everything was moving in slow motion. My head was in a perpetual state of numbness. My mom was standing at her bathroom sink, staring down at a tube of lipstick that she couldn't decide whether to wear. I inhaled, slow and deep, through my nose. That was when a realization hit me like a cold slap across the face: the smell of my dad was still in that room. Not the smell of hospital soap. Not the smell of his clammy chemo-sweats. Just him. I hadn't smelled *him* in so long that, breathing it in nearly overwhelmed me into a panic attack. Since then, when I *have* to go in there, I try to breathe strictly through my mouth.

I tiptoe towards the closed door and lean forward, just barely pressing my ear to it. The box fan that Mom can't sleep without whirs inside. Slowly, gingerly, I wrap my hand around the doorknob and turn it, careful not to make a sound. I crack the door just enough to peek in with one eye.

Mom is in bed. Still asleep, breathing deeply. Wrapped in her arms and pressed to her blotchy, tear-stained face is my dad's pillow. I see that she is wearing one of his favorite flannel shirts.

I silently close the door and walk back towards my room. I feel the divide between my mom and me, like a canyon, widening.

CHAPTER SIX

The weekend passes in a blur.

Then Monday passes in a blur.

Then Tuesday.

Wednesday.

My mind is in a perpetual state of fogginess that I can't seem to shake. I get up every morning. I come to school and do all the stuff that feels mundane even when I'm *not* like this. I go home, exist parallel to my mom, tend to the plants in the greenhouse, go to bed, and then it's lather, rinse, repeat.

I try to push Tony out of my mind.

I *fail* to push Tony out of my mind.

I mentally kick myself for becoming a girl who can't even pass the Bechdel test in my own mind.

In my defense, it's not like he's making it easy to avoid thinking of him obsessively, though, in my defense. He hasn't been at school all week. While that fact *should* shake me out of at least the Tony-tainted element of this fog, it's having the opposite effect.

Absence makes the heart obsess more.

Thursday at lunch, my friends finally say something.

"What's going on with you, you stoner?" Laura asks.

I am startled out of my stupor and blink at her like a deer caught in headlights. "Huh?" I ask dumbly.

"You've been acting incredibly stoned all week, and we all agreed that if we started smoking weed, we'd share!" She shrieks in mock-hysterics.

I stare at her flatly for a second, then reply, "I'm not smoking weed."

"You *have* been acting a little off, though," Alondra pipes up kindly, "is everything okay?"

"She's high off her ass!" Laura laughs.

I cut my eyes at her, quickly becoming frustrated.

"God, Laura," I say, my voice dripping venom, "I almost wish I *was* high. At least then I wouldn't have to actively remind myself every five minutes why anyone here talks to you when you make everyone around you so miserable."

Laura's mouth falls open and a hush falls over the lunch table as she and I stare at one another. Her eyes are wide with shock. Mine feel full of fire.

"Out of all of us, Tulip's probably the last person who would smoke weed. Well, her or Val." Reagan says to Laura after a long, awkward silence.

"Well then, who would be the first?" Stephanie

asks her.

We all look at her pointedly.

A laugh erupts from her suddenly, sounding like a witch's cackle. "Okay, that's fair." She says.

I look from her to my torn-up and uneaten sandwich. Thankfully, I am no longer the group's subject of concern for today. Only Val remains looking at me, her brows furrowed in concern.

After school, I make a beeline for the greenhouse. It isn't even that the plants need tending to today, it's that I need to be in their presence to ground and soothe me.

I close the greenhouse door behind me and sit on the tarp floor. I look around me at all the succulents, the lilies, the orchids, the spider plants, and the ferns in their pots of various shapes and sizes.

I am surrounded by green beauty.

I let my eyes drift closed and inhale slowly through my nose. I let the smell of wet potting soil and the hints of fragrance from the various blooms around me fill me like air in a balloon. Slowly, it feels like a tension inside me is being released. I feel the thump of my heart in my chest slow. I can fully feel and enjoy every breath as it goes into my nose, down my throat, and into my chest, then back up again and out from between my lips.

For the first time all week, I find myself able to clear my mind and think of nothing other than the sensations of *now*. I feel the rough, lumpy ground beneath the tarp under my butt and legs. I feel my back slouching into an almost C-shape and consciously straighten my spine, popping at least one vertebra and opening my lungs to more of the earthy, damp air. Slowly, gently, and easily, I feel peace.

And then I hear the crunch of a footstep outside the greenhouse, on the dry weeds that surround it.

My eyes snap open, and I jerk my head right and left to try to see through the tempered glass, but I see nothing. Still, I work to control my breathing so as not to make a sound as I listen for more sounds. All I can hear is the pounding of my heart in my ears, but I try to push past that to listen for another sign that I am not alone out here.

It's then that my gaze falls to the plants.

Every single one of them is suddenly facing me. The lilies are all opened in my direction, and so are the orchids. Even the spider plants, all the different succulents, and the Boston Fern have a look like their individual fronds and leaves are leaning towards me, the way they would lean towards a light source.

My brow furrows and I look around at all the plants again. Sure enough, they all lean and open in my direction from wherever they are in the greenhouse. I rise to my feet slowly, not taking my eyes off the plants around me as if they are a bear that could attack as soon as I stop looking. I think of the optical illusion that some people see in old painted portraits, where the eyes of the sitter follow you from one side of the room to the other. That is what I see in front of me, only the plants keep their gazes on me, rather than a nameless, painted person.

I turn back towards the greenhouse door and

freeze. I can't make out specific features, but through the textured glass of the door, I see a figure. Slightly taller than me, and standing a few feet back from the door, is the slender frame of a black-haired person, clad all in black. My breath hitches in a gasp as I feel the intense tickle of recognition in the back of my mind.

It's *her*. In my yard. Outside my greenhouse.

"H—hello?" I call out, my voice shaking.

She doesn't move. She doesn't reply.

"Can I help you with something?" I try, forcing myself to be louder, firmer, more confident even while my face tingles in total panic.

Again, she says and does nothing.

I gulp. I begin to wonder if maybe I'm hallucinating. That can happen when you spend too long in a humid environment, right? I'm pretty used to the greenhouse, but maybe I'm dehydrated?

It's faint, but the movement is enough that I catch it despite my growing panic. A tilt of her head to the side. She's there. She heard me. She sees me. She's studying me.

"What do you want?!" I shriek.

Without turning away from me, I see through the door as she backs up, out of my range of visibility. I hear a low chuckle just before she's out of my sight. I jerk my hand on the doorknob and push it open roughly. I expect to see her closer to the house, but instead, all I see is the house. I look around the yard and still see no trace of her.

For what is probably the first time in my life, I run at full speed until I make it through the back door and into my bedroom, where I plan to remain until morning.

The mirror.

The hallway.

Weeping.

Music. Sad, mournful, beautiful music. Played on strings of some kind.

I float towards the mirror.

Two hands, emerging from darkness. Strong, thick hands. Holding something. A ball. They dig their nails into the ball and split it open. It's a pomegranate. Juice drips down the fingers into the palms.

I float closer to the mirror.

The hands come closer, holding out the pomegranate halves to me.

An offering.

A promise.

Love.

My shape begins to form in the mirror. It's blurry. I float closer.

Love?

I am speeding at the mirror. My image growing

larger in it.

Awaken!

With a gasp, I roll out of my bed and fall onto the floor. The sound of my morning alarm plays obnoxiously on my phone above me on the bedside table. I reach up and grab it. I silence my alarm and let my hand plop back down onto my chest, feeling my heart racing as I take a deep gulp of air.

Val, thanks to my mom being called in last-minute again, picks me up to drive me to school today and makes what she calls a mandatory coffee stop to, as she says, "put some pep" in my step. I slide down into the passenger seat, to-go cup of iced coffee in hand, and rest my eyes.

"So," Val starts with a tone of trepidation, "is everything okay with you?"

I open my eyes and turn to look at her in confusion. "What do you mean?"

Val sighs. "Look, I didn't like how she

approached it yesterday, but Laura *did* have a point at lunch. You haven't been acting like yourself this week. What's going on?" She takes her eyes off the road to glance in my direction for a second.

I look away from her and straight ahead. "Nothing's going on." I lie.

In truth, there is definitely something going on with me. But I don't know what to call it, and I feel stupid at even just the thought of having to verbalize that to her. I've felt off since my *moment* with Tony last week, but it's been much longer since I've felt right, and I can't blame that on Tony.

I used to glide through life under the assumption that everything would always work out for the best of everyone. I used to have an ease that carried me and made me feel weightless. Nowadays, it just feels like my body is on autopilot, going through the motions of my daily tasks.

Tending to my plants brings me something resembling the old lightness I used to feel, but it's fleeting. As foggy as my brain has been the last week, and as frustrating as it's been having nothing but Tony, Tony, Tony on my mind, a part of me has to admit that it's been refreshing. It's somewhat of a relief that I've at least been feeling *something* other than the dread of needing to talk to my mom about next year.

"Then… Care to explain why you went off on Laura yesterday at lunch?" Val asks.

I instantly feel my face grow hot. Was I harsh with her yesterday? There's no doubt about it. But I've never matched her harshness the way I had yesterday.

"I know she was being… Well, Laura," Val presses, "but you usually laugh her off. I'm not saying she didn't deserve to be chewed out—because she did—but that's just… *So* not you, you know? You're not mean the way she is. You're the person who tries to make everyone feel good about themselves!"

I say nothing and offer only a shrug.

Val sighs again and I look over at her once more. She gives me another glance before turning her eyes back to the road. "I just want you to know that I'm here, okay? If you need to talk... About *anything*. You're my best friend, and I'm here for you."

I gulp. I take a sip of my iced coffee and blink back tears. I'm at a loss for what to say for a few minutes.

"I know," I finally reply, in a voice just above a whisper. "I don't know what I'd do without you, Val."

At school, I make a conscious effort to put myself back into Normal Tulip Mode. In English, Val and I convince Mrs. McMyres to let us work on our essays' Works Cited pages in the hallway, where we sit on the floor and gossip more than we do actual work. In my other classes, I chat with classmates I'm familiar with and laugh at their jokes. By the end of the fourth period, I'm even making some of my own jokes. By lunch, when I'm sitting with my friends and actually eating the food in my brown bag for once, I almost feel like the version of myself that I was at the beginning of last week again.

But then I hear a familiar voice behind me saying, "Hey Tulip."

I feel my face suddenly grow hot as my friends all look at him. I turn around in my chair and look up at Tony. I gulp down a bite of my sandwich that seems to have suddenly solidified in my mouth. "Hey, Tony," I say, quietly.

"Where have *you* been?!" Val asks him excitedly next to me.

He rips his gaze away from mine to smile weakly at Val. "Been sick this week, but my moms said I couldn't miss another day." He looks back at me and says, "Can I talk to you?"

I take a slow breath in, wanting—*needing* to go with him and talk, while also wanting to cling to the slight normalcy I've forced back into my life today. "Okay." I surrender, rising from my seat and following him out of the cafeteria and towards the library.

He leads me to an alcove with a bench built into the wall, turning and having a seat before looking up at me expectantly.

I hesitate for a beat but decide to sit on the bench

with him, not liking the feeling of hovering over him. I cross my arms over my chest, unsure of what else to do with my hands, and turn to him, waiting to find out what he wants to talk to me about.

He looks at me, and I feel immensely vulnerable as soon as we make eye contact. It's like he can see *into* me as easily as he can see just what's in front of him. His eyes aren't harsh or searing; in fact, there's a softness to them as he pierces my soul. My cheeks feel so hot right now that I think I'd melt an ice pack in seconds.

"Hey." He finally says to me.

"Hey," I reply awkwardly, "So... What was it that you wanted to talk to me about?"

Tony looks away from me and off into the distance, sucking in his lips thoughtfully. I study him while his attention is elsewhere, finding that I feel my heart flutter as I let myself soak in the details of him, from the texture of his hair to the soft glow of his smooth skin, to the length of his eyelashes. I feel like I could study him forever and never get bored.

He startles me by abruptly looking back at me, his eye-contact immediate and intense as he says: "I want you to come somewhere with me."

I furrow my eyebrows in confusion. "I—I *did*...?" I stutter in confusion, "I followed you over here to talk?"

He breathes out a laugh. It isn't mocking, it almost sounds embarrassed. "I meant like somewhere else. Off-campus?"

"Oh," I say, feeling my forehead relax at the clarification. "Um, okay. After school today?"

He bites his bottom lip and raises his eyebrows, sending me a nonverbal signal.

"Oh," I say again. "You mean now*?* But we're in school!"

"It's *one* afternoon," Tony says, "You won't miss anything."

"Except, like, three classes!" I exclaim. I have never, in my life, left school early without a valid reason. My heart races at the mere suggestion. How would we walk past the front office without getting stopped? What if my mom sees us in town? Unlikely, since she's supposed to be working late yet again, but still.

"Please, Tulip," Tony says, interrupting my spiraling thoughts. My eyes focus back on his and I see sincerity and seriousness in them. "It's important to me that you come with me right now. I want to show you something. I won't let you get in trouble."

I stare at Tony, my mouth slightly agape. I could say no. I should say no, probably. I am not someone who skips school. Especially with a boy. If Mom found out, she would absolutely kill me. I wouldn't have to worry about having The College Talk with her.

But, looking at Tony right now, I know that I am going to go with him. It will undoubtedly make me paranoid from the time we leave until graduation day that I will get caught and expelled for it, but I can't *not* go with him. Not now, not with the yearning ache I feel in my heart just to be in his presence for as long as I can.

"Okay," I say quietly. "I just need to get my backpack."

He smiles. "Meet me out front. I'll pull my car up."

With that, he stands and walks towards the front of the school. I watch him, having a perfect view of the front entrance where I sit in this alcove. He walks with such confidence that, even if there were any adults over there, I'm sure they wouldn't stop him.

Suddenly, the bell rings. Lunch is over. I hear the scrape of chairs magnified by a thousand as everyone in my lunch period gets up to leave.

I stand, knees shaking in fear of what I'm about to do. I walk back to where my friends and I sat for lunch. I see they've all left, except for Val. Someone—probably her—has thrown away the lunch I left behind, except for my water bottle, which I only took a single sip of. Val stands by the table, holding my backpack in one hand, smiling at me as she raises it to hand it over.

"What did Tony want?" She asks cheerfully as I sling it onto my shoulders.

"Um," I say, suddenly finding myself unable to look her in the eyes. "He actually wants me to go somewhere with him right now." I roll my eyes to look up at Val while my face is still downturned.

She jerks her head back slightly in surprise. "But… we're at school?" She lets out a confused, breathy laugh because I know she can't believe what she's hearing.

"Yeah," I say, "It's just the last three classes, though. And really only two that I ever do anything in, so…"

She tilts her head at me. "Tulip, you're about to *skip*?" I hear the deep concern in her voice. "You *never* skip. What could be *so* important—"

"It's just this one time," I say, cutting her off. "I just feel like I *have* to do this, okay?"

I don't give her time to respond. I turn on my heel and walk towards the front entrance to meet Tony outside.

Val doesn't follow after me, but the last thing I

hear before pushing through the doors to the front of the
school is her calling my name.

CHAPTER SEVEN

Tony and I sit in his car in total silence for the first ten minutes of this ride. We both keep stealing glances at one another anxiously.

I'm the one who breaks the silence out of sheer desperation to diffuse this clear tension. I clear my throat and ask: "So, where are we going?"

"You know the nature center?" Tony asks.

"Well, yeah," I reply incredulously. Years ago, some rich ex-actress randomly decided to retire in our town and funded the establishment of a 75-acre nature center on the opposite side of town from the high school. She named it the Lucille Nature Center in honor of her late mother.

At the nature center, there's a small cabin with a window unit AC with one wall entirely made of thick glass for birdwatching, a modest hiking trail shrouded in looming Oak trees, and a massive garden divided into patches of gorgeous native flowering plants of all different colors. Over the years, it's become *the* spot in town where countless family photos have been taken.

Tony shoots me a lopsided smile. "Well, that's where we're going."

"But, why?" I ask, exasperated.

He lets out a chuckle and brings his attention back to the road.

"Tony!" I bark.

"Chill, woman! Patience is a virtue. You'll find out soon enough." Tony doesn't look at me, but I hear the amusement at my expense in his voice.

Fifteen minutes later, we pull into the parking lot

of the nature center. Tony parks in the corner of the lot, unbuckles his seat belt, and turns to face me wordlessly.

I turn to face him, waiting.

We stare at one another like that for a beat. Then, Tony opens his door without a word and gets out.

I huff. When I see he's already walking without me, I scramble to unbuckle and chase after him. Because Tony is so much taller, I have to jog to catch up with him, while he is walking at a somewhat brisk pace. He leads us away from the parking lot and towards the garden area. I think about asking him again to explain something—*anything* about what we're doing here, but I think that will be about as successful as the other times I asked him for an explanation. So, I follow him in silence.

We pass the birdwatching house and enter the garden by walking under the arbor at its beginning. Tony leads me onto the footpath, and it feels immediately like the garden swallows me whole. Colors and fragrances surround me on every side, from the tall magnolia blossoms on one side of me, the Texas Mountain Laurel on another, the Black-Eyed Susans reaching out to touch my left knee, to the patch of Scarlett Sage that looks like each stem is twisting so that the flowers can get a good look at me.

I slightly slow my pace, awestruck at the sight of it all. It's almost too much to take in at once. It's been years since I've been here in this garden, and I can't help but gasp at its beauty now.

Finally putting my attention back on Tony, I see that he's stopped just a few yards ahead of me. I come to a stop next to him, looking up at his face, which is fixed ahead of him. I see his shoulders rise and fall as he breathes deeply. His hands are in his pockets, and I wonder if it's to hide the fact that they're shaking.

Because mine are shaking.

As desperately as I want to be with Tony right now, and as much as I need him to give me an explanation for all the weirdness of the past week and release me from the fog it's put me in, I suddenly feel my stomach clench with anxiety. I don't know how I know this, but I am certain that everything is about to change between us.

"Are you going to tell me what this is all about now? Please? What's going on with you?" I ask quietly

Tony sighs deeply and turns his body towards me. His eyes are wide, earnest, and burning into my soul through mine.

"Okay," he says in a soft voice. "I'm going to ask you to do something. And it's probably going to feel weird that I'm asking you to do it. But just trust me, okay? I promise, it's going to make everything make sense."

"Tony!" I say sharply, louder than I meant to. "Enough with being cryptic! All I know is that a week ago, everything was fine, everything was normal, and you had some weird episode in class that's just... Just screwed everything up!" The pitch of my voice has risen. I take a slow breath to calm myself enough to bring it back down.

"Look," I continue, voice much more even, "I don't know what happened, but I know that things feel really… weird between us. I can't stop thinking about you, and about this weirdness between us, and I want to understand what happened. I want to understand why."

"I know," he replies solemnly. "Believe me, I know. And I'm going to help you understand why. That's why I need you to listen to what I'm about to ask you to do, okay? I need you to trust me. If you trust me, I'll be able to help you understand. I didn't have help, and it was terrifying. I don't want it to be like that for you. So, trust me."

I stare up at him, willing his rambling to make even just a little bit of sense. I can't make it happen. But I also know that, right now, I can't make myself say no to whatever it is that he's going to ask me to do—short of committing a murder or doing drugs, anyway.

I sigh, my shoulders slumping. Wordlessly, I nod at him.

He sucks in a breath through his teeth, then looks ahead of us again. "You see this bed of flowers here?" he asks me.

Stretched out before us at about knee-height is a large patch of white poppies.

"Yeah," I say.

"I need you to go stand in the middle of it," Tony says. He looks back down at me. "About ten steps away or so."

"I can't do that," I protest, "I'll trample them and kill them!"

"They'll be fine," Tony insists. "You can watch your step if you want, but you won't hurt them. Just ten steps."

I suppress the urge to roll my eyes by closing them instead. I take a quick breath, then mutter a begrudging "Okay," and step off the footpath and into the flower bed.

I try my hardest to avoid stepping on any stems, practically walking on my toes through the crowded bed of poppies. When I'm ten steps away from where I started, I turn to look back at Tony.

He nods. "Okay," he says in a voice loud enough

for me to hear him from this distance. "Now turn away from me, okay?"

I jerk my head back in surprise and look at him incredulously, "Seriously?" I say.

"Trust me."

I'm not loving his apparent mantra of the day. With another sigh, I turn my back to him.

"It was confusing at first," Tony says from behind me. "I panicked when it first happened. I didn't know what was real and what wasn't... I thought I had gone crazy or something."

"What was confusing?" I ask him, not turning to look because I don't want him to see how quickly I am breathing.

"The memories," Tony says. "*So* many memories. It was like... Like when you remember doing something when you were a kid. You can picture it clearly, it's almost like a movie in your head, right? But then your mom says that it never really happened, or it wasn't you that did that. But you remember it being you that did it, you know?"

I open my mouth to reply, but nothing comes out. I kind of understand what he's saying, but it isn't clearing up anything that I need him to clear up for me.

Tony continues: "That day in class, it was you. I saw you and it awakened all these memories of us in my head. Only not us *now*, it was the way we were back then."

"Tony—" I say, starting to shake all over in fear. What is he saying? What am I doing here?

He doesn't stop talking. "And when I remembered, I couldn't believe that I hadn't remembered all along. That I hadn't recognized you the whole time. You'd been so close to me this whole time, and I couldn't believe that I hadn't realized it."

My knees feel weak. My heart slams against my ribs inside my chest. My breaths are fast and shallow. My face is cold and tingling.

"It was your hair," Tony says, "the way it flipped when you turned to look at me real quick. It was just like back then. It *made* me remember."

Without warning, a loud, brittle *CLACK* rang through the air.

I whipped my head around to face Tony, who still stood ten steps behind me, one large round stone in each of his hands, held above his head where he just clapped them together.

The hallway.

Tony lowers the rocks and his movements are sluggish.

The mirror.

Tony is farther away from me now, but he hasn't moved.

A field of poppies.

He drops the rocks. They fall slowly, like through water. I cannot move.

The earth is opening up.

He takes a step towards me. The sky around me

is suddenly dark. All I see is Tony, walking towards me, through a bed of white poppies.

Red poppies.

White poppies.

I float closer to the mirror.

My vision strobes. He is coming towards me. His lips are moving. All I hear is my wheezing, quick breaths, and my pounding heart, and a ringing, ringing, ringing.

The memories, I think.

The pomegranate. An offering.

Voices echoing all around me. *So* many voices. Weeping.

Tony's voice.

Tony is getting closer. He is Tony. My vision flickers, like my brain is blinking. He is taller. Older. More broad-shouldered and thick-chested. He is Tony again.

Another flicker. He is the other man again.

Black eyes. Black as a moonless night sky.

So… many… memories.

Green eyes. Tony.

I am in a field of red poppies. I am picking them and placing them in a basket. I hear the earth open. I turn and see him in a flash. I feel his arm around my waist from behind. I am pulled downward.

It's me. But not Tulip.

I begin to fall backwards. Tony is in front of me now, his hands on my arms, steadying me. He is speaking. I hear only my breath, my heart, and that ringing.

I am beneath the earth. It is cold.

I could be the queen here.

"You're okay." I hear Tony's voice, faint as a whisper, through my breathing, my heart, and the ringing.

He holds out the two halves of the pomegranate. "You don't have to stay. You don't have to choose this. Or me," I hear him say through my breathing, my heart, and the ringing, "but if you want to be my queen, there is a way…"

He loves me. He is letting me choose. But not Tony. Not Tulip.

I approach the mirror at the end of the hallway. My form in it starts to sharpen. I see myself.

Not Tulip.

My face. I remember this face. It was so long ago.

I am Tulip now. But I wasn't then.

I am in a bed of white poppies. Tony is in front of me, grasping my arms, holding me upright. With a *whoosh*, the ringing stops.

"I remember," I gasp, tears streaming down my cheeks, "I remember." A sob rips out of me and shakes my entire body.

Tony—but he isn't *just* Tony; I know that now—hunches down until we're eye-level. "Do you remember who you are?" he asks softly.

I can't stop the sobs now. They're coming from somewhere deep inside me

I nod.

Then, in a voice that is almost a croak, I say: "I'm Persephone."

CHAPTER EIGHT

Tracy Burns gave birth to Tulip Lorelai Burns at 7 PM on a Monday with her husband, Jack, holding her hand and smiling on. I didn't know the details of that night until this afternoon, but I do now. I see it in my mind like any other memory.

I also see other memories. Older ones—thousands of years old. I see the flowers I used to give life to, sprouting up from the earth. Some of them don't even exist anymore, and I can see them so clearly in my mind that I feel as if I could reach out and touch them. I see the souls of the dead lined up in front of

Hades and me, waiting for judgment. I hear the sobbing of those who died by violent ends.

I don't remember everything. But I will eventually. I don't know how I know that; it just feels inevitable. Was this how it was for Tony?

I have been in bed since Tony reluctantly dropped me off.

No. Not Tony. Not *only* Tony.

I am Tulip. But not *only* Tulip. I know that now. I never have been.

But I *am* Tulip... Aren't I? I can remember being born into this body. I was born to my parents. I remember them teaching me to feed myself, teaching me to walk. I remember my dad teaching me how to ride a bike and being excited to teach me how to drive. I remember my dad being diagnosed, being told that there was a high survival rate, that his cancer had been caught early. I remember the fear I felt that I was going to lose him. I remember the way I wanted to rip the heart out of my own chest just to stop the pain when the nurse told my mom and me that they'd lost him, the ringing in my ears and the feeling that the walls of the hospital around us were collapsing.

I remember my mom dancing with me in the living room to a pop song and the laughter that we'd fill the room with when I was little. But is she even really my mom? Was he really my dad? How can I have two sets of parents? Because I do have two sets of parents, don't I? I have Tracy and Jack *now*, but I also had—have—the parents from before, too.

I remember the Before. I remember the end of it all a little easier than I remember anything else so far. So long ago. We were worshipped once. People made offerings to us in temples.

I helped to take care of human souls for eternity; Hades and I found them new homes in our world… Places to rest.

People would pray to us. They would beat their fists on the ground to get our attention, begging us to hear their most desperate cries.

And then the offerings stopped.

First mine, and then the ones to Hades.

The prayers slowed and quieted.

The souls stopped coming to us. We didn't know *where* they went.

Of the two of us, I faded first.

I just… stopped being.

And then, I was reborn.

My phone vibrates on my nightstand. It has done so at regular intervals for the last two hours, ever since school let out. I haven't checked it. I don't need to check it to know that it's Val. It's Friday night, and I should be at her house right now.

But I can't.

Val is my best friend. She knows me so well that she can always tell something is off just by how I text her. I can't face her; she'll know something is wrong, and for the first time in my life—this life—I have a secret I can't share with her. She would never believe me, or, if she somehow did believe me, she'd be scared of me.

I can't stand the thought of that.

I hear a sharp knock on the front door. Mom still isn't home, and I didn't order anything for dinner, so I choose to ignore it. I have too much swimming around in my head to deal with a solicitor at the moment. My phone vibrates again, this time repeating to show that it is a call, rather than a text.

Another knock at the front door.

The continued *buzz* of my phone.

The buzz of bees hopping from flower to flower in the field as I walked, picking them and placing them in my basket.

I throw my blanket off me and practically leap out of bed at the flash of memory. My senses are overwhelmed by the noise consuming me. My heart races like I woke from a nightmare. I hear the knock again.

Letting out a growl of frustration, I fling my

bedroom door open and stomp to the front door, yanking it open. I freeze.

"So, you've lost your phone?" Val says accusingly, "Or are you just ignoring me?" She lowers her own phone from her ear and hits the End Call icon.

I gape at her.

Her face softens, but only slightly. I'm still in the Hot Seat. "You're letting bugs into your house." She says before pushing past me and coming inside.

I close the door behind her and follow her as she walks toward my living room, as comfortable in my house as she is in her own. "Val, I—"

She turns on her heel and cuts me off: "Y'know, I don't judge you for skipping this afternoon. I really don't. Sure, it's out of character for you, but it's our senior year, and you've had a really hard one so far. I don't judge you for skipping with a guy, because it's Tony, and we *love* Tony. If the two of you wanted to ditch so you could go somewhere and goof off, hook up, rob a bank, *whatever*, then more power to you! But you know what I can't wrap my head around, Tulip? You know what actually pisses me off?!"

I say nothing. I can't even look her in the eyes. I cross my arms and shift my weight to one foot and let my gaze wilt to the floor.

"It's that you won't talk to me!" Val answers, "After everything we've been through together, all the secrets we've always trusted each other with, I have no idea what's going on with you! It would be one thing if you said, 'I'm not ready to talk about it, Val', or even 'I don't *have* to tell you everything, Val', because you don't... I get nothing! And now you aren't even answering my calls or texts? When all I've ever done is try to be a good friend?"

I hear a hitch in her voice and risk a glance at her. Sure enough, tears are brimming her eyes. I know Val, though. She's going to fight them like her life depends on it.

"You are a good friend," I mumble, letting my eyes dart away from hers again.

"Then just *tell* me," Val says with desperation creeping into her voice, "What's going on with you?"

I can't tell her. I would sound insane. When I review the facts to myself, knowing all that I know, even I think I sound insane. She's always been my safe person, the best friend I've ever had, and I've told her things I couldn't even trust my parents with. But I can't tell her this.

After waiting through my silence for far longer than I think anyone else would, I hear Val sniffle. Without another word, she walks past me towards the front door. I turn and watch her go, her head held high. She opens the front door and pauses, but doesn't look back, then she leaves and closes it gently behind her.

Feeling heartbroken, I drag my feet back to my room. I'm about to lie back down when I hear my phone vibrate yet again. I look down at the screen. Above all the notifications I ignored from Val is a text notification from Tony.

Meet me outside in ten. It says.

CHAPTER NINE

"Where are we going?" I ask before I've even closed the passenger door all the way.

"I just thought we could go for a drive," Tony says, "and buckle up."

"I'm thousands of years old," I spit out bitterly, "I'm a goddess. Why should I buckle up?"

One corner of Tony's lips quirks up sympathetically. "We don't know that these bodies are immortal like our old ones. Don't be a brat."

Begrudgingly, I fasten my seatbelt.

"Do you want to go anywhere, or is it alright with you if we just drive around?" Tony asks as he rolls his car down my street.

"Well, that depends," I reply, "do you plan on traumatizing me anymore today? Have any other things in mind that I need to ruin life as I know it by remembering suddenly?" My voice is sharp, but I don't care. This morning, I was seventeen years old and my biggest problem was trying to be honest with my mother about my dreams for the future, and now... Well, I'm still seventeen years old, but I'm also thousands of years old too, and I have a whole other set of parents and a whole other life I lived before mankind was past its infancy. And I'd be lying if I said I'm not angry at Tony for making me remember it.

Tony sighs. "I'm sorry," he says, looking at me briefly. "I know, it was... A lot. It was for me too. I just... couldn't stand the thought of it happening to you while you were alone or something. I wanted to be there for you to help you through it, if you needed."

I narrow my eyes at him. "Oh, I'm sure there was nothing selfish or self-serving about your decision to handle it the way you did," I say, my voice dripping with sarcasm.

His mouth quirks up into a slight smile. "Maybe there was an element of selfishness, too, yeah."

I roll my eyes, but I feel my justified anger towards him lessening. Can I honestly say I wouldn't have done the same thing if the tables were turned?

"So, I take it you know why it was selfish of me, right? You remember who I am?"

I look at him and feel heat in my cheeks and the flutter of butterflies in my stomach. "Yes," I whisper.

He looks at me again. "Then who am I, Seph?"

The name he used to call me before. I feel my heart tighten at the memory, and *all* the anger I felt toward him just seconds ago completely melts away. I am filled to the brim with all the centuries-old love we shared. The fact that our souls came to life again so near to one another... well, what are the odds?

Tony pulls the car into the deserted parking lot of an old gas station and fixes me with a stare, waiting for me to respond. His eyes are pleading with me to confirm what he hopes to be true. My eyes drift to his lips, and I feel like I need to catch my breath.

"You're Hades," I whisper, so softly that I'm not completely sure he can hear me. I look into his eyes. "My husband."

His lips part ever so slightly with the breath he had been holding in. Relief loosens his features and his eyes look glassy. I feel the sting of tears in my own as I continue to look at him.

His eyes—his old eyes—were the last thing I saw before I faded. His voice reassuring me was the last thing I had heard. He looked so different back then. His eyes were black, his skin was a darker, warmer umber, and his hair was longer and in dreadlocks. He was thicker and taller then, but I guess that makes sense. He hadn't been born into a mortal, human body. As beautiful as he is now, he was a marvel to see then.

He raises a hand to stroke my cheek. I lean into

his touch, a gesture so familiar to me now that I practically do it out of muscle memory, and close my eyes at the feel of his soft, warm skin against mine. I breathe in slowly through my nose, smelling his body spray but remembering the earthy, metallic way his skin used to smell. I open my eyes and for just a second, I see him as he used to be, when he was God of the Underworld. Then that image fades into the Tony I've known for the last ten years of this life; the lean, lithe boy with brown skin, dazzling green eyes, and a smile that could light up the world.

"Come here." He whispers in a low, smoky voice before leaning towards me.

I lean in and close my eyes.

Our lips touch each other. Soft and warm. It feels like coming home. It's tender at first, but then Tony brings his other hand to my other cheek to cup my face, and I wrap my arms around his neck and pull him as close to me as I can while we're both still held back by our seatbelts, and our kiss becomes urgent, frantic, and starved.

We kiss like that until we are both breathless, and we press our foreheads together.

"I *needed* you to remember," Tony says. "Knowing that you were right here… That after all this time, we found a way to each other again… I couldn't wait another second, and I didn't want to risk you having to go through it alone. I shouldn't have rushed it, and I'm sorry for how that had to feel."

"I get it," I reply. "I don't know if I would have done it any differently than you did."

We pry ourselves apart, but he laces his fingers through mine.

"I'm sorry you had to go through it alone," I say softly.

"Oh, I didn't go through it alone." He says. "Well, I mean I did at the beginning of it. But then I got help for pushing through it."

I furrow my brow at him in confusion. "What do you mean?" I ask.

"Well, it started when we were in class, right?"

Tony says, "But then when I was in the nurse, I heard her voice in my head telling me to meet up with her outside so she could talk me through it."

"Her?" I ask, shaking my head slightly.

"Oh, Nyx," Tony says. "And Moros too. They felt it when I… I don't know, awakened? And they came to help me."

My jaw drops in realization.

The girl in black outside the greenhouse. No, not the girl in black… The goddess of night. The night itself. Nyx. She had been there, watching me, waiting. And her son, Moros, was the guy Tony saw outside his house, and probably who was with Tony and Nyx the day Tony remembered that he was Hades.

"Where is Nyx?" I ask. I have so many questions I need to ask her. Why are we back? *How* are we back? What does all this mean?

"No idea." Tony shrugs.

I gape at him, appalled. "You didn't ask where she'd be, how we could find her?"

Tony purses his lips and gives me a blank, wide-eyed stare.

"Well did you at least ask why this happened? How many of us have come back? How many others have awakened already?" I demand.

Tony shakes his head. "I didn't really think to ask any of that."

I raise an eyebrow at him. "You're serious?"

He smiles sheepishly. "You were always the more inquisitive one. But we don't need to go to her. She'll come to *us*. You'll probably see her before too long now. She feels it when one of us awakens. Well, I guess we all feel it when one of us awakens. I felt it when it happened to you."

"You were *there* when it happened to me." I remind him.

He laughs, "I mean, I think I would have felt it even if I wasn't there, you know what I'm saying? It was like... I dunno, like a tickle in the back of my head."

I nod. "I know exactly what you mean."

An hour later, after a lot more talking and a lot more kissing, Tony drops me off at home again as the sun dips below the horizon. Mom still isn't back. I let myself into the house and turn on the front porch light for her.

I stand in the entryway for a beat. I feel unsure of what to do with myself. At this time on a usual Friday night, I'd be with Val. We'd have already gone to the convenience store to get a bunch of junk snacks and decided on a scary movie to watch. But Val and I aren't going to have our usual Friday night sleepover tonight. I don't know if we'll ever have our usual Friday night sleepover again. Val is furious with me, and I can't blame her. Even if she ever stops being furious with me, I don't know if things can ever be the same with us now that I know what I am.

But I can't think about that now. That, on top of all the other questions and memories currently swimming through my mind is just too much. I have to think of something else. I have to do something other than think about all of this right now. Before, I could always distract myself with creation, with my plants. I guess, at least in that way, I'm the same now as I was then.

I look down the hall, across the house, at the back door.

The greenhouse. An idea strikes me

I hurry out back and into the greenhouse, barely making sure to close the back door behind me in my rush. I throw the greenhouse door open and tear into my gardening supplies. I get a pot and haphazardly toss it onto an empty shelf. Then I find the bag of soil and my trowel and shovel heaps of the soil into the pot until it's filled almost to the brim.

I let the bag and the trowel plop down on the ground by my feet. I'll pick it up in a second. My eyes are zeroed in on the pot or earth in front of me. I place my hands on either side of it, holding it a lot like how Tony held my face in the car. I take a deep breath in and close my eyes.

I picture a seed in my mind as I let my breath go, a tiny, teardrop-shaped, brown seed. The image in my mind is so sharp, I feel I could pluck this seed out of thin air. I feel a pull deep within my chest. I breathe in again and change the picture in my mind ever so slightly; now the seed is splitting in half, on the edge of the big curve. A round, soft, pale curve comes out of the split.

The pale curve turns green and pushes free.

A second petal joins the first… heart-shaped. A thin white stem follows.

The seed dissolves. The stem lengthens.

Two new leaves unfurl.

More leaves. Their edges zig-zagged and pointed.

The stem thickens and darkens. Roots are pushing downward into the soil. The plant stretches higher.

The shoot in my mind reaches a foot tall.

I hold that picture in my mind, feeling that pull from within myself connecting with the pot between my hands.

Slowly, I open my eyes and allow the picture in my mind to dissolve into what is in front of me.

I let out a soft breath.

In the pot I hold is the seedling of an apple tree, almost ready to be transplanted into a bigger pot. The exact seedling I pictured in my mind. I have created a new apple tree.

From nothing.

"*There* she is," a rich voice cuts through the silence from behind me.

I whirl around, a gasp caught in my throat.

The girl is here. In my greenhouse. She's wearing dark gray and tastefully ripped and frayed jeans, Mary Janes with ruffly white socks peeking out at me, and a form-fitting black long-sleeved shirt. Her black shoulder-length bob is smooth. She stands casually with her weight on one foot, her hands in her back pockets. Effortlessly chic in a gothic way.

"Nyx," I breathe.

CHAPTER TEN

Nyx smiles at me, but it doesn't touch her eyes. "Persephone," she responds. "I was wondering how long Hades would hold out. I told him to let it happen naturally, but you know him." She lets out a chuckle. "How are you feeling, Little Springtime?"

I open my mouth, but all that comes out is a small, almost inaudible croak.

Nyx nods, her eyebrows raised in a gesture of sincerity. "You must have a lot of questions. Take your time."

"I—" I struggle to find my words. I do have a lot of questions. Where to even begin? I look at my new apple tree, then back at her. I hold the pot up in front of me as if I'm presenting it and tell Nyx, "I made a tree."

Her eyes flit to my creation briefly. An amused smile touching her lips. "So you have." She replies.

We stare at one another for a while as the greenhouse grows darker. I study Nyx, trying to remember what she looked like before, but I'm failing to conjure up an image. It's probably one of the billions of memories that will come back to me eventually. The Nyx in front of me now is slender, and taller than me by about six inches. Her eyes are a wintry, piercing blue and thoroughly lined with pitch black, tastefully smudged eyeliner. She has a classic heart-shaped face with high cheekbones and a daintily pointed chin, further accentuated by her short hair. It's impossible to guess how old she is in this life, but I would venture to guess she's in her early twenties.

Nyx snickers, though it sounds like she's trying to suppress it. "Shall I start with some of the Frequently

Asked Questions, then? Afterward, you can ask any follow-ups."

I gulp and nod as my cheeks redden. I must come across as a real idiot to her right now.

She nods back and leans against the shelf behind her. "Well, for starters, you are a goddess. You know that much already. You are the goddess of springtime and queen of the Underworld. A long, long time ago, you and your husband ruled an entire realm together—the ultimate realm, really—and you, on your own, were at least partially in control of the seasons and vegetation."

"I know that already," I start, but Nyx silences me with a quick lift of her palm towards me.

"You were honored, revered, worshipped, adored, blah, blah, blah," Nyx continues, "until a funny little fella named Paul brought new lessons and practices to our people." Her face darkens and her eyes look beyond me, staring into the distance. "All of a sudden, our people weren't our people anymore. They didn't honor us. They didn't give us the respect or the admiration we are entitled to. They came up with all sorts of alternative ideas about the way things worked. They believed they didn't need us anymore. Eventually, they forgot us all together." Nyx takes a sharp breath, and her eyes come back into focus on me. Her tone is lighter again. "Well, you know what happened next."

"We faded," I say.

"We faded," she confirms. "Turns out, that's how you kill a god. You forget them."

"But if we died," I ask, "then how is it that we're... Here? Why are we back?"

She smiles. "An excellent question." She says. "If the way to kill a god is by stopping your rituals and offerings to them, no longer praying to them, and forgetting them, can you guess how you can revive a god?"

I look down at the plant in my hands. "Well," I say, looking back up at her, "you'd start praying to them again. Making the offerings. Remembering... Right?"

"Exactly, Little Springtime," Nyx says triumphantly.

"So, you're telling me that people are praying to me again? People are making offerings in temples to me again?" I raise an eyebrow at her incredulously.

"It looks a little different these days," Nyx says, laughing at me, "people have their own altars in their homes now. No need for temples anymore to call upon us."

"I haven't heard anyone calling upon me," I tell her flatly, "I haven't received any offerings."

"Well, you wouldn't have yet, would you? You were only just awakened hours ago. You'll hear the prayers again soon enough, and you'll be able to collect your offerings. Your little sapling there is just the beginning."

I place the pot on the shelf behind me and turn back to her. "So," I say, "I'm able to do all the things I used to do now?"

Nyx sighs, "Not all the things you used to do. Not yet. But soon, yes. I'd say judging by what you've done tonight," she nods toward my tree, "your skills will come back to you quickly. Some of us have been able to do a watered-down version of what we used to for a while, even before awakening. Aphrodite has always had people fawning all over her in this life without her having to do anything particularly special." She rolls her eyes and practically snarls. "And your beloved husband used to have a lot of imaginary friends when you two were small, right?"

I furrow my brow and nod. It's true; when Tony and I met in elementary school, we would play lots of playground games that involved carrying one imaginary friend of his or another somewhere safe, or calming them because they were scared. No matter what the scenario was, we were always taking on the role of caretaker to them. I think back to one of those times, remembering it with vivid clarity. We were each on one side of an imaginary friend he had named Robin, our hands up as if we were both guiding Robin by the hands, together. Only now, I see something in my raised palm in the memory. It doesn't look like a hand, exactly. And it isn't attached to anything really human-looking—just a faint, silver, shimmering haze, almost like a thin cloud floating between Tony and me.

"Those were souls." I whisper, almost inaudibly. The realization hits me like an anvil has been dropped on me.

Nyx's lips widen into a Cheshire grin, and she nods. "The two of you were taking care of the untethered strays before you could even comprehend it. Kind of sweet, huh?"

I stare at her, my mouth hanging open.

She continues: "You'll probably be seeing more of them before too long now too. Hades has. It seemed like he fell right back into the routine. But that's more his area than yours. Especially at this time of year. Your gifts have always been more in line with what you've already been doing." She takes a look around her at my plants, which are now painted in the shadow of night.

"How many of us are there?" I ask, "That have been awakened, I mean?"

Nyx opens her mouth to answer, but on the other side of the house, I hear the squeal of my mom's brakes as she pulls into the driveway.

Nyx hears it too and stands, making like she's going to leave.

"Wait," I say with an edge of panic in my voice, and I have to stop myself from reaching out and grabbing her arm. She turns to me, one eyebrow raised.

"Um," I say, feeling embarrassed to be so worked up when her demeanor is so cool, "do you have, like, a cellphone or something? Some way I can reach you? I have so many more questions, I—"

Nyx cuts me off: "You've had a long day. Get some rest. You haven't seen the last of me, Little Springtime. You can count on that."

And with that, the goddess of night leaves my greenhouse.

CHAPTER ELEVEN

My greenhouse is bursting with life. I've filled
every shelf and even parts of the floor with blooms from
nothing. Vines climb the walls, though not enough to
block out the light. Every time I step in there to tend to
them—which has become a twice daily routine—every
plant turns and opens up to me in greeting, like a baby to
its mother.

It's been a month since my awakening.

One whole month since I remembered who I am.
Since *we* remembered who we are.

Tony has been by my side almost constantly. If my mom were to ask—which she hasn't—I'd probably say he's my boyfriend, even though neither of us have ever used that word or even discussed it. "Husband" feels... Truer, but also not quite right. I know we're gods, but I'm not sure what the rules of marriage are when death (or something like it) actually has parted you at least once. Plus, I'm still seventeen for the next two months, and referring to him that way is just a little too *Law and Order: SVU* for my personal taste.

Our time together has been filled with returning memories and power. A lot of kissing too, because we have literal centuries of not getting to kiss to make up for. As Nyx predicted, Tony's been seeing more and more souls. For him, they seem to be a lot clearer, but I sometimes see them too, flickering in and out of the world like fireflies waiting to be guided. Tony has been much more helpful to them than I have so far.

On one particular Wednesday evening after school, Tony had driven us back to the nature center. His fingers were laced through mine as music blasted from his car's speakers. We didn't say anything for the entire car ride, but it was a comfortable silence between us. Each of us basking in the presence of the other, continually stealing glances at one another and then shyly looking away when we made eye contact.

When he pulled into the parking lot, we lazily strolled towards the garden where he awakened me. His arm was around my shoulders, and he kept pulling me close to him to plant passionate kisses on my lips that stopped us both dead in our tracks.

It took us at least twice as long to get to the garden than it would normally have.

We sat among the flowers— this time, a patch of purple verbena— Tony behind me with his arms propping his torso up, his legs stretched out in front of him, and me sitting between them with my back leaned against his chest.

I closed my eyes and felt the warmth from the sun on my face and the warmth from his body on my back. The chittering of squirrels and buzz of insects filled the air around me while Tony's heartbeat rapped gently against the back of my head.

"Do you see him?" Tony whispered suddenly.

My eyes eased open. I looked up at him to see his eyes pointed to our left, fixed on a point far away. I followed the trail with my own eyes, but saw nothing.

"Is it a dead person?" I asked him, my voice coming out as a whisper too, despite us being the only living people here.

I felt him nod and I once again focused my attention on the spot in the distance that held his. I narrowed my eyes, willing the soul to become visible to me the way it was to him.

After what felt like forever, I was finally able to see… something. It didn't look like a person. It didn't really look like anything at all, except maybe the stray sparks from a fading 4th of July Sparkler.

"Do you need to go help him?" I ask Tony with a sigh, feeling defeated at not being able to make out more of this soul.

"Nah," Tony says with a shake of his head, "he's not quite ready yet. He hasn't worked out that he's dead yet. Once he does, then I'll be able to help him."

I didn't know what Tony meant by that. I didn't know what it meant to help the dead at all. I had been focused only on my own powers and the growing connection I felt to plants and to nature. It had always been a quality I possessed, but now that my past self had been awakened, I felt like I lived for it. I had a hard time feeling particularly interested in helping the dead when I still couldn't even see them.

As if reading my thoughts, Tony said, "I bet you'll be able to see them when we get to the Fall. It's almost summertime right now, but you only ever came to me when your mother *had* to let you," despite my back being to him, the bitterness was evident when he mentioned Demeter, my old mother. "So, you wouldn't have seen them this time of year."

A monarch butterfly drifted through the air from a nearby flower then. I tracked it with my eyes until it touched down gingerly on my thigh. I reached towards it and tenderly scooped my index finger under its feather-light legs and lifted it closer to my face. It flapped its wings slowly, not to fly away, but to let the sun warm them.

"And here I was, starting to feel bad about not being able to see them. I thought maybe I wasn't trying hard enough or something," I said. "Actually, I think it's fair to say that I haven't really been trying at all. I just like my plants so much more," I grinned at the last sentence and glanced up at him to see him fighting a grin of his own.

On my hand, the butterfly started walking the length of my finger, turning to try and find the best angle to get warm.

"I think that's why we've always been so perfect for each other," Tony said in a soft tone, "you love life so much. And the living. You love it so much that it fills you up... it gives you a different understanding of the dead than even I have."

"And you have an understanding of death that makes it less scary," I replied, "it gives you compassion. It makes death seem less like... like the scary skull-man in a hooded cloak and more like a friend you haven't seen in a long time."

"We work so perfectly together because we create balance," Tony agreed, "Life and death... One can't exist without the other," he lifted his hand towards mine, where the butterfly was trailing towards my knuckle. "And I can't exist without you. Not in the way I should, anyway."

Tony's index finger touched the back of my hand. The butterfly walked from my knuckle to his finger. It made it halfway up the length of his finger before I lowered my hand. Then, I watched as the butterfly froze where it stood, its wings no longer flapping lazily. Its little legs curled in on themselves, and it fell slowly from Tony's finger to my lap, drifting side to side like a piece of paper in the air.

All the time I've spent with Tony has been a necessary distraction from the fact that my friends and I haven't felt right since I remembered. No one has said anything about it, at least not to me, but there is a very clear divide between me and the rest of them. I can tell that they talk about me when I'm not around. Val and I have been orbiting one another politely, tensely, since that night. She's tried acting like everything is normal… And I guess I have too. But it's been awkward. We haven't even mentioned a Friday night sleepover in this entire month. Of course, to have mentioned it, we'd have to be talking, which we barely do.

I miss her.

Last week, I was the last one to our lunch table. She doesn't wait to walk with me anymore.

Everyone was laughing when I reached my usual spot and sat down.

"What's so funny?" I had asked no one in particular.

Everyone's laughter faded and they all looked at one another pointedly.

Alondra had been the one to finally answer me. "It's nothing honestly. Levi just isn't taking the break-up well. Steph was reading us some of the texts."

I turned to Steph. "Wait, you and Levi broke up?"

She scoffed at me. "Yeah. Like forever ago."

I had looked around and everyone had been avoiding looking at me. Laura was looking at Val with raised eyebrows. Val had been looking back at her but let her eyes drop to her lunch when she felt me looking at her.

No one had said anything directly to me for the rest of that lunch period. That was the last time I ate with them.

Mom hasn't seemed to notice any change, which is good. I hate lying to her. She and I really only interact now when she takes me to or from school, which hasn't even been all that often anymore. She's picked up more shifts at work and by the time she gets home, she's apparently so exhausted that she goes straight to bed. Tony has taken on the role of my chauffeur, which is just fine by me.

Except, of course, when he has track meets after school, like today.

Rather than wait at the school for him to finish, call my mom and ask her leave work early, or face the awkwardness of asking Val for a ride home, I decide to walk to the town square. It's just under three miles, but there's a bookstore there, along with an assortment of boutiques and small businesses.

143

I've remembered so much about my past already, but there are still so many gaps that I want to fill. I don't want to wait.

An antique bell hanging over the door lets out a cheery ring as I walk inside the bookstore. It smells like an apple cinnamon candle in here. While it's no Barnes & Noble, this bookstore is impressive in both its physical size and selection.

A smartly dressed woman with a gray pixie cut, cat-eye glasses, and fierce red lipstick stands behind the counter. She smiles so wide at me that she almost looks like a puppet.

"Hi! Welcome in! Anything I can help you find, Hun?" Her accent is more country than a biscuit. She is nice, but a little too much for me.

I smile politely back at her. "Oh, no thank you," I say, "just browsing."

"Well, you let me know if there's anything you need. I'll just be right up here!"

I nod and walk past the counter as she goes back

to tapping her long, thick, cherry-red nails on the iPad at the register in front of her. Luckily, the sections in this store are clearly marked.

Near the very back of the store, through a cozy sitting area littered with children's books and floor toys, I spot a sign for *Folklore and Mythology*. I walk past the rows of shelves and stacks, passing only a few people on the way, until I see a portion of the shelves dedicated to Greek Mythology. All the titles are basically the same, so I pick a thicker book with the brightest colored cover. I flip through the pages, skimming the pages for my name. Well, my *old* name.

I stop when I finally find it.

A chapter called *The Abduction of Persephone*.

I read through it, finding that while some things match up to my experiences, it doesn't tell the story very accurately. For one thing, I wasn't held captive like this story suggests. But then I realize that, for a story that claims to be about me, I'm actually not a very active player in the story. It's mostly about how Hades conspired to kidnap me (I roll my eyes at that) and the fallout of *his* actions. I'm little more than a damsel wearing a flower crown.

I close the book and place it back on the shelf, then pick up another. I repeat the process of skimming for my name. I find a story of my birth, but—again—I barely exist in it.

I sigh and shelf the second book.

As I reach for a third book to try and find missing pieces of my story, I hear a gasp behind me.

I turn and see a woman staring at me, her mouth partially open and her eyes wide. She looks to be in her thirties or so, with some faint wrinkles on the corners of her eyes and a little extra tummy in her middle—hidden under an oversized T-shirt—that just looks like what tends to get left over after having a baby or two. Her hair is thin and only slightly darker than strawberry blonde and seeing her instantly gives me that tickle in the back of my head.

I lower my arm and turn toward her, cocking my head. As I open my mouth to ask her if I know her, my vision of her shifts. The woman in front of me flickers and is replaced by a taller woman, her skin smoother and more bronzed by the sun, with golden hair that has what looks like a crown of wheat laced through it. I blink rapidly and let out a gasp of my own.

"Mother?" I ask in a whisper.

CHAPTER TWELVE

We sit across from one another in a coffee shop two doors down from the bookstore.

"So..." I say, tapping my fingers on the table across from her—my first mother.

She sighs and nods. "So..."

In our past life, she was Demeter, the goddess of the mortals' agriculture and harvests. She took care of them by helping with their crops and keeping them fed. In our new, modern life, she is Sadie-Mae Camlen, a library assistant and mom of two.

I stop my finger tapping and sit up straight. I lean toward her with a raised eyebrow and tell her: "I never would have guessed I had an Other Mother when I was little. Good thing you aren't built like a spider, huh?"

She straightens, eyebrows shooting up in surprise before bursting into laughter. Her laugh is sudden and booming. A few heads in this coffee shop turn, but no one looks annoyed. They smiled, like the sound of her laughter brightened their day a little.

I laugh too. I can't help it. The way she throws her head back and clutches her chest, laughing with such abandon. It stirs something up within me— joy and belonging. I feel instantly comfortable in her presence.

Her laugh slows to an occasional chuckle. "Oh," she sighs, "you and my oldest would get along. She loves that movie."

She pauses, blinks, then corrects herself: "I mean, my oldest *now*. God, it's still so hard wrapping my mind around this… I mean, I know I'm Demeter. But I'm also Sadie, you know?"

"I know exactly what you mean. Tony—uh, Hades—keeps calling me my old nickname, Seph. But I sometimes don't answer right away because I still feel like Tulip."

She sips her iced coffee. "Is he still going by Tony, or are you calling him Hades?"

I sigh. "I call him Tony. Calling him Hades now, after spending so long calling him Tony just doesn't feel accurate. He doesn't correct me or anything, but I get the feeling that, the way I feel about being called by my old name? That's how he feels about being called by his new one."

She nods. "To be fair, his old name is shorter than either of ours'. Easier to get out of one's mouth." She chuckles.

I laugh. "Yeah, I guess that's a good point."

I take a bite out of my chocolate croissant then ask her: "So, how old are your kids? My... Sisters?"

She smiles but her eyebrows are drawn together. "Oh wow, yeah, I didn't think about that... You are kind of their sister, huh? So weird."

I shrug, "If you don't want me to refer to them that way—"

She shakes her head, cutting me off: "Oh no, no, no! It's not like that. I don't mean it's weird because of *you*, I—"

Now, I shake my head. "No, I understand. It is weird. Like, biologically we're not… really related anymore? In the mortal way, anyway."

"Right," she nods, "But… you are my daughter still."

"Yeah." I smile softly at her. "And you're my mother."

She smiles back at me and agrees: "Yeah. Anyway, umm… Well, I have two girls. Anna is five, and Leah just turned two. Anna is *obsessed* with unicorns and spooky things. Leah is a total wild child."

"Cute!" I say, "Can I see a picture, or… is that weird?"

"Not weird at all," Sadie says, pulling her phone out of her back pocket and scrolling through several pictures in her camera roll. The girls are very cute. Both have full heads of red hair in different shades. Anna's is darker than Sadie's and Leah's, and is thick, long, and curly. Leah's looks more like Sadie's, straight, thin, and more on the strawberry side. Anna's eyes are dark brown and penetrating, while Leah's are a carefree, light blue.

"Wow, they're adorable!" I gush as she puts her phone back in her pocket, smiling.

"Thanks," she replies, "It's funny. I didn't notice until I held their pictures up to show you, but you actually look like you could be their biological sister. How funny!"

"I was thinking that too, actually! I'd love to meet them someday, if that's okay."

"I think that can be arranged," she replies, grinning at me. "But enough about me! Tell me all about you! I want to know all about your new life and the kind of young woman you've been becoming for the last seventeen years!"

We talked for hours. She asked me questions about my childhood. I told her about Mom and Dad, about Dad building the greenhouse in the backyard, about him getting sick. I told her about the distance that's been growing between Mom and I since he died. I told her about Val, and about Tony—how he'd been before we awakened.

She asked me about my favorite books and what I want to do after high school. I asked her about her memories from Before, and she told me things I hadn't yet remembered for myself and was a lot more informative than the books that I tried finding answers in. We laughed together. She teared up listening to me talk about my dad.

It wasn't until the sky outside turned pink and the barista started stacking chairs on the tables around us that we realized how much time had passed. She offered to give me a ride home, and I accepted. I didn't want our time together to end.

Before I get out of her car, we make sure to

exchange phone numbers. I also follow her on all of her social media just for good measure. I walk up my driveway, past Mom's car and put my phone back in my pocket before I enter the house.

I hear sounds coming from the kitchen area.

"Mom?" I call out, surprised to arrive home and find her awake.

"I made some mac and cheese!" She replies.

I drop my backpack into my bedroom by the door and make my way to the kitchen. She's still in her scrubs. She scoops a large spoonful of the food into a bowl and hands it to me. I take it and sit at the table.

Mom sighs as she joins me at the table with her own bowl. I eat my macaroni quietly, replaying my entire meeting with my other mother. I feel my insides humming with excitement at having met her, at having been able to spend some time with her. She listened to me so excitedly—both of us feeling like a missing part of ourselves had been found again.

She doesn't live here, but the next town over, and

just happened to be window shopping on the square when she felt pulled into the bookstore. She said she'd had no idea what she would find in there, but that she knew it would be wonderful. I'm so glad to have met her.

"I was thinking," Mom says, startling me out of my train of thought, "prom isn't too far away. We should go shopping for a dress for you! Just you and me, or you could invite Val. I always love having her around."

I stare into my macaroni as I stab my fork into the elbow noodles. "Umm, sure. That could be fun. I don't think Val will want to come though, considering we aren't talking."

Mom's head jerks back in surprise. "Since when?"

I raise an eyebrow at her. "For, like, a month now, Mom." I say that last word much sharper than I intended it to be. "Haven't you noticed that I've been here every Friday night?"

Mom opens her mouth to reply but no words

come out. Her gaze drops to her own bowl of macaroni. "I guess not." She mumbles.

We spend the next few moments in silence before she tries striking up a conversation again: "Hey, maybe over the summer we could give your room a make-over. Make it more college-friendly. You don't have a desk, and you'll need one for studying and homework, right? I mean, you can always do that stuff here at the table, but it might be nice to be able to step away from the books for little breaks."

I feel my stomach drop. I put my fork down into my bowl and cross my arms in front of me on the table. I look at my mom. I feel like I am out of breath. I squeeze my biceps to keep my hands from shaking.

"What if I live in a dorm? That would make the room make-over kind of a waste." I hear the slight quiver in my voice. I feel icy heat rising my neck and into my cheeks.

Mom blinks at me in surprise. "Oh, I just thought since Edgecreek is so close there was no sense in paying for you to stay in a dorm."

"Well," I say slowly, trying to contain the anger suddenly boiling inside me, "that's another thing. What if I don't go to Edgecreek?"

"But… You got in so long ago… I thought—"

"I got accepted into three different schools, Mom," I snap, "I never said I was going to Edgecreek. I only even applied there because you thought I should. Just to be safe."

Mom furrows her brows at me and opens her mouth to respond, but I cut her off again: "And then when I got accepted, that was good enough for you! You didn't even care when the other acceptance letters came in! You acted like it was a done deal!"

"It has one of the best pre-dentistry programs around, Tulip," Mom says in a small voice, "I just thought—"

"Mom, when have I ever said I wanted to do that?! I mean name one time I've expressed interest in being a dentist—and not that one time when I was six years old—name one time I have said that that was what

I wanted to do!"

Mom's mouth hangs open and she stares at me. I see tears brimming in her eyes and I look back down at my mac and cheese. She has raised me. She lives in the same house as me.

And I can't remember the last time she actually asked me what I wanted. What my plans were.

I've been worried about how she'd react if she sensed the change in me since I awakened, but why? She hasn't even noticed that my best friend and I aren't talking. She hasn't noticed that it's been Tony taking me to and from school. She knows nothing about me. She doesn't get me, and she doesn't care enough to get me. I spent hours with my other mother, who hasn't even known me in this life until today, and in those few hours, she made more of an effort to know me than the woman who raised me has.

"Tulip, I'm—"

"Forget it. I'm full. Thanks for dinner." I say, and I jump from the table and go to my room for the night.

CHAPTER THIRTEEN

Nyx wants to see us.

I rub my sleepy eyes to see the text from Tony clearly.

It's three in the morning. I left my mom at the kitchen table hours ago and have been shut away in my room ever since. I heard her footsteps approach my door at about ten, but she turned around and went to her room after only a few seconds. My light had been on, and she would have been able to see that from under the door.

Now I've been pulled from my sleep by this text

from Tony.

It takes me a moment for the message to sink in, but when it does, I sit up straight in bed and text him back: *Now? Where?*

I watch his dots impatiently until his reply comes through: *I'm coming to get you, be outside in five.*

I leap out of my bed and dress as quickly and quietly as I can, throwing on a pair of sweatpants and a T-shirt with tennis shoes. I run a brush through my hair and put it in a ponytail, then tiptoe silently from my room and out the front door, locking it behind me.

As promised, Tony's car appears and pulls over in front of my house within five minutes. I hop in and greet him with a quick peck on the lips.

"So, where are we going to meet her?" I ask as I buckle my seatbelt.

"Not sure yet." Tony replies. His voice is thick with exhaustion.

I look at him, my face screwed up in confusion. "What do you mean? She didn't give you an address?"

160

He shakes his head in reply.

I jerk my head back. "Well then hand me your phone. I'll text her and ask."

"I don't have her number."

"You don't have her number," I repeat back at him, slowly, my confusion growing. "So how did she tell you she wants to meet up?"

He taps his head and glances at me.

"Hey, Mr. Mime, I'm gonna need some actual words here."

I see Tony suppress the urge to roll his eyes as he takes a deep breath in. "I felt her calling to me. You can probably feel it too."

I look ahead to the road in front of us. Can I feel Nyx's call? I listen to my body, and after a moment, I feel the tickle at the back of my head. The same tickle I've felt every time I've seen Nyx, and when Sadie found me in the bookstore. I close my eyes and focus all my attention on that tickle.

I allow it to grow in size until it feels like my whole head is being pricked by needles, like when my foot falls asleep. My mind is full of the sound of static. Somewhere within the noise, I hear a voice—commanding and powerful, but in a silky-smooth, quiet way, like a cat's purr.

It says only one word: *Come.*

I open my eyes and look at Tony. "Oh, that's creepy!"

His mouth quirks up in a smile. "Not real helpful. I'm kind of picking the direction we go on gut instinct."

I raise an eyebrow at him.

He shoots me a look and says: "Look, I know it sounds nuts, but I just kind of... *know* which way to go."

"Okay then," I say slowly. "Normal. We are two totally normal people doing totally normal things."

He chuckles, and then we are silent for the rest of the drive.

Eventually, Tony pulls the car over to the side of

a completely deserted backroad. There are no streetlights, so I pull out my phone and turn on the flashlight. There haven't been any homes or businesses for at least five minutes since we turned on this road, and there are so many potholes along the way that I feel it's safe to assume that the county forgot this place long ago. On either side of the road are weedy ditches and a line of unkempt trees.

Tony takes his phone out for the flashlight too, then reaches for my hand. I lace my fingers through his and we start fighting our way through the weeds and into darkness and the trees.

When we're under the cover of the trees, I feel a pull like what Tony described. It's like I know where to go without understanding *how*. After a few minutes of dodging branches and roots, we hear hushed voices. We follow the sound and come to a small clearing where three people wait, their phone flashlights already on.

One of the people is Sadie. She's wearing an outfit eerily similar to mine, except in Ugg slippers instead of tennis shoes. She smiles warmly at me as we

163

approach, and I return the smile.

Another member of our impromptu posse is a woman that's definitely older than me, but it's hard to say by how much. She's possibly Sadie's age, maybe a little older. In the flashlight glow, I can see that she has thick mascara on, or possibly false lashes, and shimmering lip gloss. Her honey-blonde hair is twisted into a perfectly messy bun on top of her head, and she's wearing a pink tank and shorts athleisure set. The past overlays the present in my vision for just a moment, and I recognize her—Aphrodite.

The third person is a guy who looks to be in his mid-twenties. He's tall and lean, with muscles obvious under a fitted white T-shirt and low-slung black pants. His jawline is sharp enough to cut glass, and his sandy hair—clearly highlighted—is cut to frame his face. He looks like he's ready to jump into an Abercrombie ad. As he gives me a slow and deliberate once-over, I can see who he is—Ares.

Sadie comes over and wraps me in a warm hug. I let go of Tony's hand and allow her arms to swallow me.

164

Tony approaches Ares and they give one another a handshake that turns into a bro-hug—the kind that ends with a mutual pat on the back.

Aphrodite approaches Sadie and me as we separate. She offers me a tight-lipped smile. "Heeeeeyyyyyyy." She says to me in a long, high-pitched, obviously uncomfortable tone.

I give her a stiff and uncomfortable smile of my own. "Hi," I say, then I point to myself and add: "Tulip."

She nods and mimics my gesture, saying: "Tatum."

Tony and Ares approach us. I nod my head towards Tony and tell Sadie and Tatum: "This is Tony."

Tony looks at Aphrodite and clarifies: "Hades."

Ares looks directly at me, his gaze penetrating. I squirm and inch closer to Sadie.

"You all already know who *I* am," he says, "but my new name is Logan."

"Good, I won't need to do your introductions."

We all jump at the sound of Nyx's voice.

She and the guy I saw with her when she spoke with Tony stand behind us. I can tell by the way we all startled that no one heard them approach. The beams of all our lights go towards them. Nyx waves her hand in front of herself, and the lights all grow dim. Seeming to understand all at the same time, we point our phones down to the ground as a group. Nyx smirks and the brightness of our lights all increases again.

The lights are all pointed down but is enough so that we can all still see her, dressed in all black as usual. Her face is so pale in contrast that it seems to glow like the moon.

I study the guy that's with her. He looks roughly my age, though his angry face ages him up a little. I can tell from the usual tickle that he's one of us, but I seem to have no memories of him from the past to fade in and out of my vision, so I can't tell which one of us he is, but he must be Moros.

"You've all awakened somewhat recently," Nyx begins, addressing us as a group, "but you feel it, don't you? The emptiness where others should stand. This is just a sliver of what we once were, but the others will awaken too. You all just happened to live relatively close to one another in your new lives. An incredible coincidence."

Sadie and I look at one another, and Tony weaves his fingers through mine and gives my hand a tender squeeze.

Nyx continues: "It would be one thing if we were only weaker in numbers. We can work with that. We'd still be able to find the rest of our large *family* with ease if that was all it was. We are, unfortunately, also weak in power."

I raise my hand.

Nyx cuts her eyes at me. "Question, Little Springtime?" she says thinly.

"Well, you said we're weak in power," I reply, "but we do have powers. I've been making plants from nothing, just like the old days, and Tony—"

"Those are parlor tricks compared to what we

used to do!" The guy with Nyx spits, stepping up to stand squarely beside her, his eyes burning into me.

Nyx smiles and places her hand on his back. "My son, Moros," she says to all of us, "I don't believe anyone here ever had the privilege of meeting him in our previous life."

The guy—Moros—nods once in greeting, casting a polite glance at everyone else, but his simmering glare is back on me immediately. I avert my eyes, giving Nyx my full attention to try and diffuse whatever slight I've committed against him.

Nyx clears her throat, then resumes her speech: "We are weak in power currently. It's true that we can do *some* of what we used to nowadays, but it too is just a fraction of what it once was. What we lack… is divinity. That's why I called you all here."

She looks at Moros, who finally takes his angry stare off me to read her expression. He grunts softly and gives her a curt nod before taking something out of his back pocket, then squatting down low on the ground.

"You all should remember this. It came to us a little differently back in the old days, but the taste is still as sweet as ever."

With her speech apparently finished, Nyx looks at Moros again. He opens the item he pulled from his back pocket to reveal that it was a knife.

Moros holds the knife in his right hand and opens his left hand wide. Quickly, he swipes the blade of the knife across the open palm. I take a sharp breath in through my teeth as his blood flows instantly to the open cut. He tilts his hand to let the blood drip into the dirt in front of him. Thick drops hit the ground one by one until they form a small pool. The rest of us stare at the pool curiously.

Beneath me, I feel the ground hum through my tennis shoes. The earth under us vibrates with energy, the vibration traveling into me from the soles of my feet, filling my body in a warm rush.

"Do you feel that?" Sadie whispers to me.

Before I can answer, the pool of Moros's blood in

the dirt starts bubbling. It's slow at first, and then quickly turns to a full boil. Then, from the center of his pooled blood, emerges a thick, dark green, vertical line.

A stem.

The stem grows until it's about six inches high, and I watch as two leaves unfurl from around it and open wide.

Then, from the top of the stem, a bud. It starts as about the size of an egg, but soon I can see distinct petals that open into the shape of a teacup.

Each petal is white, with a silver, almost glittery sheen. From the center of the opened flower comes a glow.

It starts small—little more than a glimmer—but quickly grows to fill the entire teacup shape of the flower and glows in a vibrant gold hue. The glow shines through the porcelain-white petals and I can see gold, glowing veins through them.

The flower *radiates* power. Even the air around it shimmers.

The flower pulsates like it has a heartbeat. I can feel it through the earth even though I'm at least six feet away from it. I'm filled with wonder looking at it, and a little bit of fear. When I grow the plants in my greenhouse, I feel a pull coming from within myself, like my heart itself is tugging the sprouts out of the ground.

But right now, it feels like something is being tugged *out* of me by this flower.

Sadie and I look at one another, and I can tell from the way her eyebrows are knit together that she feels it too.

"The Chrysantheion flower," Nyx announces to all of us, drawing our attention back to her, "is what gave us our Nectar before. Some of you may remember that, in addition to feeding *us*, it could also heal, or grant powers to the mortals we decided were worthy of it. Now, it is what will restore our divinity."

She nods to Moros, who reaches down and plucks the flower off the stem, careful not to spill the glowing gold nectar. He raises the flower to his lips and throws it back in a gulp. The flower, now empty, falls to

171

the ground.

Moros stands, squaring his shoulders and closing his eyes. All of us who were summoned here tonight are holding our breath.

Then, I see it.

Beneath the surface of his skin, a slowly growing glow radiates outward.

I hear Tatum gasp.

Logan claps his hands together once and lets out a half-laughed "Oh, *shit*!" I glance at him and see he is smiling with his mouth open and his eyes wide.

Moros opens his eyes, and in his pupils are bright gold sparks, making them look like two lightening bugs.

The glow coming from within him brightens. He straightens. He looks taller and stronger, suddenly more than human.

"And now," Nyx breathes, "we have a god… *fully* restored to power."

CHAPTER FOURTEEN

"Only *you* can summon your Chrysantheion flower," Nyx informs us. "It's taken Moros weeks of tirelessly cultivating his powers—limited as they were by his mortality—before he could do this. But now, as you all see, that mortality is gone."

I study Moros. Outwardly, he doesn't look that different. He *does* look a little like a human glowstick, and yeah, the extra height and muscle are kind of intimidating… But otherwise, pretty much the same.

"Okay, but… then what?" Tatum asks.

"What do you mean?" Nyx asks, failing to hide her irritation.

"I mean, what do we do *after* we're restored? We get to live forever again, but… then what?"

"We rule over the mortals," Moros answers in a growl of a voice, "just like we did before."

"Each of us tending to our own realms," Nyx adds.

"What, from our *houses*?" Tatum asks incredulously. "We functioned on, like, a totally different plane of existence in the old days."

"What is your point, Aphrodite?" Nyx snaps.

"I think what she's trying to say," Sadie offers, "is that… Well, we *live* among the mortals now, Nyx. The home we once had is gone, isn't it? Won't it cause problems for us if we just go around glowing like that?" She gestures to Moros, then adds, "I remember that being something we actively tried to avoid, once upon a time."

"I can disguise myself just like I could back

then," Moros barks. Then, as a demonstration, he seems to shrink back down in size, and his divine glow from within fades. Nyx smugly glances from Tatum to Sadie.

We all silently exchange looks. I squeeze Tony's hand. He isn't looking at me. His stare is trained on Moros. His lips part slightly, and his gaze remains unblinking. His face, a mask I've never seen before, hides his every thought.

"Well," Nyx says, finally breaking the silence, "I've taken up enough of your time tonight. Get some rest. Spend some time meditating and honing your powers. Your instincts will kick in. Soon, you'll know how to summon your Chrysantheion. I'll call everyone back here in two weeks. First, we reclaim our divinity. Then, we find the others and give them back theirs. Then, we take back what was taken from *us*."

"What about Zeus?" Tatum asks suddenly.

Nyx pauses, faintly lifting an eyebrow before she collecting herself again. "What *about* Zeus?" she asks.

Tatum sighs and rolls her eyes. "I just mean…

He's, like, our leader. So… has he been awakened already? It feels like we need to find him before we do anything else, right?"

Everyone looks at Nyx, waiting for her response. Moros scoffs. As for Nyx, one corner of her mouth slightly quirks up. Condescendingly.

"Hasn't come back yet," she says curtly. Then, to everyone else: "see you in two weeks." With that, mother and son disappear into the darkness and leave the rest of us behind for the next two weeks.

I have no reason to question Nyx. Theoretically, I have no reason not to trust her.

But I know she's lying about Zeus, and I don't know why.

Tony and I drive back to my house in silence.

When he finally parks his car at the end of my driveway, we sit there for a moment, not speaking or moving, just staring ahead.

I'm the one to break our silence: "Well, that was a lot to take in."

Tony says nothing.

I turn to him. He continues staring ahead, his hands gripping the steering wheel and his eyes out of focus, darting from one place to another as his thoughts jump around inside his head.

"Hey," I say, poking his temple gently with one finger, "what's going on in there?"

He looks at me, finally. His eyes are wide, like I startled him.

"You've been so quiet," I say softly, "what are you thinking?"

He lets out a quick breath, and the corners of his mouth slowly crawl upward into a smile. He shakes his head and replies, "I'm just... I can't believe it, you know? In two weeks, we can be *back*."

I tilt my head to the side and smile wryly at him. "We've been back, babe."

He smacks his lips at me. "You know what I mean, Seph. We'll have *real* power again! We'll be *in* charge again, like we should have been all along!" He slaps the back of one hand into the palm of the other for emphasis.

I sigh. "Yeah, I guess so."

He looks at me incredulously. "You *guess* so? How are you not completely fired up about this?"

I look away from him. What he's saying makes sense. We will be getting back what was taken from us. We will be *divine* again. Everything can be like it was before. I will have a real purpose again.

But the thing is, I'm not entirely sure what my purpose was before. All the books at the bookstore, and even the Internet searches I've done for stories of my old life, have been less than helpful in figuring out what exactly I was made for. All "my" stories don't even seem to feature me as the main character. So, it may be easy for Tony to be—as he put it—fired up about this, but maybe it would help *me* be fired up about it if I could see the point.

He always had a clear purpose, and he always lived up to it.

"Persephone?" Tony startles me out of my thoughts.

"Sorry," I say, "I'm just tired. I guess all the excitement just hit me. I should go inside and get some sleep."

He studies me but nods. "Yeah, okay. Cool. Go get some rest. I'm tired too."

"It was a big night," I say, stretching my arms in front of me for emphasis, "Can I get a sleep-tight kiss?"

He smirks and leans forward, pressing a soft peck on my lips. "I love you, Seph."

I open the door and step out of the car. Leaning down before I close it, I reply, "I love you too, Tony." I close the car door and turn toward my house.

Mom and I are tiptoeing around one another. The discomfort between us could be cut with a butter knife. All weekend, she has only spoken to me out of necessity, and there's been no mention whatsoever about college or dentistry.

Not that I've made any effort to diffuse the tension either. I certainly haven't said anything to her other than polite responses.

I bounce between my room and the greenhouse. Anywhere else feels too hostile and overwhelming because she's there. Tony's offered to pick me up and take me somewhere else, but I honestly don't even know if I want to be around him either right now. I don't want to have to talk about Nyx's plan, and I don't want to have to fake enthusiasm. So, I've mostly been ignoring my phone altogether.

In the greenhouse, I move the same pot from one shelf to another for probably the fourth time in the last half hour.

I've been out here since the sun was low in the sky. Now there is no sun. Just a soft twilight glow.

The air in the greenhouse practically hums with silence. It usually comforts me, but now it leaves me feeling unsettled as the silence presses in on me.

I glance at the door, half-expecting someone to be standing there.

There isn't, of course.

I turn my attention back to the potted plant in front of me. A spider plant. This one was formed from a larger spider plant that I created. I propagated this one and have tended to it like any mortal would. It's been doing very well, and I feel a small sense of pride, having not relied on my powers to keep it alive.

I touch the tips of my fingers to the soil to check its moisture when I feel the tickle at the back of my head.

"You've got quite the collection growing here, Little Springtime," her velvety voice croons from behind me, "no pun intended."

"Hi, Nyx," I say, not turning to her.

She glides over next to me, leaning one shoulder

against the shelf in front of me so that she is facing me with her whole body. I do not turn to face her but keep my attention on the plant in front of me.

I feel her studying my profile. "You seem restless."

"Do I?"

"You know, you were so quiet the other night when we all gathered. Of course, who could get a word in edgewise with Aphrodite there?" I see her roll her eyes in my peripheral vision.

I let out a quick breath meant to be a laugh and glance at her briefly. "Yeah, Tatum had a lot to say. Lots of questions."

I see Nyx tilt her head to the side. Then, slowly, she reaches a hand toward me. I stiffen as I feel her fingers—cool and smooth—make contact with my cheek as she sweeps a lock of my hair behind my ear. She continues stroking my hair and says, "You really shouldn't worry about the petty little disagreements and discontent with the mortals in your life, Persephone."

"How did you—"

"You're so *above* it," she continues sweetly, "you are... Spring. You are renewal. You're a goddess *and* a queen. They are nothing. You... You are so much more."

I look her in the eyes. "I don't think they're nothing."

She smiles at me pityingly while continuing to stroke my hair. "But how could they understand you, really? They have no way of knowing the *real* you, or how powerful you are. They don't give you the love or respect you deserve. They can't. They don't know how."

I look away from her and back at my little spider plant. I open my mouth to reply, but Nyx isn't finished.

"But when you summon your Chrysantheion, that won't matter," I can tell by the tone of her voice that she's smiling at me, "you'll be what you were *always* meant to be, and all of that mortal love will pour out in droves."

I shake my head, still not looking at her. "That's not—"

"And you'll have all of this with your family," she continues, "your *true* family. You want that back, don't you?"

Suddenly, my greenhouse falls away. My backyard, the house, and current reality itself fall away from me, and in front of me, I see Sadie.

Only she isn't *Sadie* as she is now. It's my mother, Demeter. Her long, golden hair flows down her back in thick curls as she leads me through a field of wheat.

She turns back to look at me. Rays of sunlight shine through her hair, wrapping around her head like a crown.

A flash. I am in bed with my husband, wrapped in his arms. I look into his black eyes. He plants a tender kiss on my lips.

Another flash. I am holding a toddler in my lap. A boy with thick, black curls. A tickle of memory in the back of my head. I *know* this little boy. He starts to turn to look at me and then—

184

Another flash, and I am surrounded by *everyone*—Mother, Hades, Aphrodite, Apollo, Athena, Zeus... We are all together.

I let out a gasp and am instantly back in the greenhouse.

I am standing face-to-face with Nyx. Her eyes bore into mine, and a smile plays on her lips. The smile doesn't quite reach her eyes.

It is fully dark outside now.

Fully night.

"You don't need them, Little Springtime," Nyx says.

"How did you—"

"*They* need *you*. And in two weeks, they will be yours to rule. In two weeks, they'll get what they need in you. In all of us." She leans forward and kisses my forehead. Her lips are cold. They stay on my forehead for several seconds.

And then, in a blink, she's gone. I am alone again

in my dark greenhouse.

I take a shuddering breath and look down at the ground where my little spider plant lies on its side, the thin white roots showing through the scattered soil lying between it and the now-broken pot.

CHAPTER FIFTEEN

For the second time in my life, I am skipping
school. I got up this morning, got dressed, and walked
out the door like everything was normal. Like I was
heading to school. Like I would be getting into Tony's
car as usual.

Except, I didn't get into Tony's car. Tony wasn't
there because I told him I wouldn't need a ride today,
and then I shut my phone off.

Instead, I walked over to the side of my house
where we have no neighbors, and I waited until I heard
Mom get into her car and leave. Then I went back inside

to toss my backpack onto my bed and made a beeline for the greenhouse.

I didn't sleep much last night, if at all. Every time I closed my eyes, I saw the visions Nyx gave me. I can't stop thinking about the way things were before we faded. I can't stop thinking about how happy I was. How at peace. How strong I felt. How loved.

Truthfully, I don't know what the big-picture consequences will be if I summon my Chrysantheion and drink the Nectar. But whatever those consequences are, I know this: I won't ever have peace again unless I get back that feeling Nyx's visions called back to my memory—the feeling of belonging to a family. She has given me a longing that I can't shake off or forget.

I *have* to get that back.

So, after leaving all my things haphazardly on my bed, I rushed out back and into the greenhouse, not even bothering to close myself inside it.

I think back to how Moros summoned his Chrysantheion. He had cut his palm and let it bleed onto the earth. But if it were that simple, we all would have done it that night. There *has* to be more to it than that.

I grab my last empty pot and pour some soil into it. Then, I dig through some of my gardening tools, looking for something sharp, but not completely filthy.

I find a brand-new pair of gardening shears still in the package. I tear the plastic apart and sit down on the greenhouse floor, my pot in front of me and the shears in my right hand.

I look back and forth between the shears and the pot.

I have no idea what to do.

Should I cut my palm and bleed into the potting soil? I *could*, but I don't want to go through the pain of cutting myself if I'm not absolutely sure it will have the desired effect.

I drop my hand holding the shears by my side and mindlessly glance around me at the floor. I freeze when I see my baby spider plant lying to my left.

The sight of it hits me like a punch in the

stomach.

After Nyx left, I rushed inside without stopping to pick it up. It looks so helpless there, its pale white roots splayed out and already drying out.

I drop the shears and pluck it up from the ground with one hand, using the other to dig a hole in the potting soil in front of me with my fingers. I gingerly tuck the roots in and cover them with the soil, then reach for the watering can at the bottom of a shelf and moisten it.

My stomach feels acidic, and I am overwhelmed with guilt that I left it lying out here all night like that. If I had gone to school, it might have died by the time I made it back out here. Sure, I could bring it back to life if I had to. I can revive any plant that's died by sheer will. But there's something so special to me about this one—this little guy I've been keeping alive with my simple gardening skills. The idea that I could have hurt it with my carelessness makes my heart ache.

I sigh and look around at all the life in here I've created and tended to. I loved my plants before I awakened, and I took good care of them. I was the certified Green Thumb of the family long before I remembered my past life. A lot of what I learned about taking care of plants was from observing my dad.

He might have built this greenhouse mostly for Mom to grow her own tomato plants, but he also liked to try his hand at growing things. Not that he was ever very successful at it.

Every time he made guacamole, he'd suspend the pit over a cup of water with toothpicks, waiting for roots. One time, it worked—until he planted it too soon. Same thing with forgotten sweet potatoes sprouting in the pantry; he'd bury them in the yard with high hopes, only for them to wither a few weeks later.

Thinking about him and his little gardening failures brings a sad smile to my lips.

I wish I had asked him more questions when he was still here. I wish I knew more about his childhood. What his dreams were when he was my age. If he ever felt a sense of purpose, or if he, like me, tended to let others point him in whatever direction seemed most appropriate.

I close my eyes and picture him. Not the pale, clammy man cancer turned him into, but the way he was when I was nine and he challenged me to a race down two side-by-side waterslides at the waterpark. He ran up the stairs to the top of the slide so quickly, his usually booming laugh coming out more like a childish giggle with excitement. He looked back at me once to make sure I was still behind him. Our eyes met, both of us grinning from ear to ear.

Tears, hot and thick, roll quickly down my cheeks at the memory. I lower my head, suddenly feeling so heavy with grief.

I will never see my dad's smile again. I will never hear his laugh fill up any room. I will never get to ask him the questions about how to navigate life and adulthood. My heart cracks open in my chest, and I let out a sob.

I cry for what feels like forever. I cry until I'm gasping for breath.

And then I gather myself. I sigh deeply and rise to my feet, leave the spider plant on the ground, and turn toward the greenhouse door. The rest of my plants track my movements as usual.

But then, suddenly, they turn their attention to something behind me. Their leaves rustle simultaneously as they shift their focus. I stop dead in my tracks, looking around at them.

And then I see a gold light reflecting off the walls around me.

I turn back to where I had just been sitting.

"Ah!" I gasp.

In front of me, in the pot where my baby spider plant had been just seconds ago, nestled in a puddle of tears, a flower blazes like it was spun from molten gold. Each petal curves like fine metalwork, catching the light in impossible ways. A low hum seems to rise from it, faint but thrumming in my bones, and the air is thick with a sweetness that tastes like honey.

My Chrysantheion.

My breath catches. It's so utterly *alive* that it feels like it's breathing with me.

My mouth hangs open. I go back and pick up the pot gently. I stare down at the flower.

I did it!

In my hands is the Nectar that will give me back my old immortality. It will make my powers unlimited. It will bring me one step closer to having a family again, with a mother who actually sees me, a husband who loves me, and a role within that family.

I lift the pot so that the flower is at eye level with me. I stare at it in wonder.

"Tulip, wait!" A voice cries out from behind me.

I swivel my head around to see two people running at full speed around the house towards me. For a second, my past life seems to merge with my current one, and it looks like Demeter and Aphrodite are gliding in my direction. Then my vision clears.

Sadie and Tatum.

"Don't drink the Nectar!" It's Sadie calling out to me.

I rise to my feet, still holding the pot with my Chrysantheion in it, and walk out to meet them.

"What are you two doing here?" I ask as they reach me, confusion tightening my features. The Nectar glows warm under my chin.

"Hon, I've been trying to reach you all weekend," Sadie pants, doubling over slightly, "why have you not answered any of my texts?!"

"Nyx is up to something," Tatum cuts in, "You remember how she said Zeus wasn't back? That was a total lie!"

I gape at her. I had sensed as much, but the certainty in her voice makes my stomach drop. Both of them stare at me with their eyes wide with urgency.

"Okay," I say slowly, glancing down at the Chrysantheion in my hands, "but… why does that mean I shouldn't drink my Nectar?"

Tatum rolls her eyes. "Girl. If Nyx is up to something—which she *is*—then why on earth would you think it's a good idea to go along with her plan?"

I pause and blink down at my flower. "Oh. Yeah, I guess that's a good point."

"We have to talk to Zeus," Sadie says, standing up straighter now that she's caught her breath.

Tatum nods emphatically. "Like *now*. And we're pretty sure we know where to find him."

"Do you want to come with us?" Sadie asks.

I glance between them for a beat, then turn back into the greenhouse. I open the door, move to the very back, and place my Chrysantheion on the bottom shelf, tucking it behind a cluster of old gardening tools. Out of sight.

I return to the others, shutting the door behind me.

"Let's go," I say.

The three of us walk around to the front of my house and pile into Sadie's car. I let Tatum sit up front, and I take the middle of the backseat, leaning forward between them.

"Where are we going to find Zeus?" I ask.

Sadie starts the car and peels out of my driveway. "It's not an exact science," she says, "but you know how we all found where to meet up the other night? Turns out it wasn't just a Nyx trick. We reached out to each other that way—"

"We both knew that Nyx was full of—" Tatum starts.

"—*so,* we figured that, if it worked with each other, we could use it to track down Boss Man himself." Sadie finishes. "We had to kind of… join forces, I guess… if that makes sense… but we're pretty sure he's at this park about forty-five minutes away."

"And if he leaves that park?" I ask.

They exchange a look. Sadie answers, "Well, with the three of us, it should be easier to find him. Let's just get there first and, if we need to regroup, we will."

I nod, then lean back in my seat. We have forty-five minutes. Might as well relax, especially since I didn't sleep last night.

After a few minutes of silence, Sadie glances at Tatum. "Did you have to call out of work?"

"No," Tatum says, "I own the salon. I just had one of my girls open today."

"You're a hairdresser?" I ask her.

She shoots me a quick look over her shoulder. "More of a stylist, but yeah." She then turns back to Sadie: "What about you? Did you have to call out?"

"Kind of. I had Dan call the library for me. I'm a terrible liar, so I figured it would be more believable if I wasn't the one pretending to be sick."

"What did you tell him?" Tatum asks.

"Who, Dan?" Sadie blinks, surprised by the question. "I told him the truth."

I lean forward again. Tatum's jaw drops.

"And by the truth, you mean...?" I prompt.

"That we're going to find Zeus," she says matter-of-factly, catching my raised brow in the rearview mirror.

Tatum and I exchange incredulous looks.

"So, your husband… like, knows about you?" Tatum presses.

"Well… yeah?"

Tatum turns in her seat to face Sadie fully. "And he didn't think you were insane? Try to get you committed?"

"At first, he didn't believe me," Sadie admits, "but he also *knows* me, you know? So, after I gave him some time to process it, he was able to wrap his mind around the whole… thing." She shrugs. "It didn't hurt that we had just *heaps* of wheat growing all around our house overnight."

I sit back, mulling this new information over. Sadie told her husband about her awakening. About what she is. And he didn't leave. He didn't even question her sanity for very long.

He believes her.

Supports her.

Could it really be possible to tell our loved ones the whole truth of who we are and have them believe us? Could I tell Val? Maybe even Mom?

I get lost in the thought, playing out conversations that have never been possible. Imagining a life where I don't have to hide the truth from the people I love most. The fantasy lulls me without realizing it, and I drift off until Sadie's voice cuts in:

"We're here," she says, the car's sudden stop jolting me awake.

Suddenly, my stomach clenches, and I can feel my heart beating in every major part of my body. I am about to come face-to-face with my other father. The king of the gods. The one who might be able to help us figure out what Nyx's agenda is, and why she's so insistent on all of us taking our Nectar.

We get out of the car and pause together for a bit. Sadie's eyes scan the park laid out in front of us. It's massive, with multiple baseball fields on one side, followed by three expansive playgrounds of differing styles stretched out beyond them, backing up to a pond that looks more like a small lake with a walking track that circles around the whole thing and leads into a line of trees.

Tatum's eyes are closed and her breathing slow and controlled.

I turn my face downward and try to tap into some inner workings that could lead me to Zeus. I slow my breathing, focusing on the air going in and out, blocking out all other thoughts. When it seems like I've blocked out the rest of the world, I call out a single word with my mind: *Father*.

I feel it radiate off me like a sonar from a ship.

Then, I feel the tickle and an unmistakable pull.

The three of us look at each other at the same time and I know they felt it too. We take off in the same direction, not even needing to say a word.

We circle the baseball fields and cut through the playgrounds, dodging small children flying down slides or running in front of us. We approach the pond and walk along its edge toward the line of trees. No one is at the pond, except for one man sitting at a bench halfway between us and the tree line, surrounded by ducks.

We are all pulled toward him.

As we get closer, I begin to make out the details of his appearance.

He is old. His paper-white hair is thinning but swept back in a classic movie star style. He wears rimless glasses over a pair of dark, deep-set eyes, underneath thick salt and pepper-colored eyebrows. His face is rounded out and covered in light wrinkles, especially around his eyes and mouth.

You can tell by looking at him that he was incredibly handsome in his prime and is still handsome in a grandpa kind of way. He wears brown loafers, khaki pants, and a dark red button-down shirt. In his hand and sitting next to him on the bench in a bag is bread, which he breaks into pieces to feed the ducks that happily quack and waddle around in front of him.

Sadie, Tatum, and I approach him. We stand shoulder to shoulder perpendicular to the bench he sits on. For a second, we all stare at him, unsure of what to say to start the conversation.

Before any of us even has to come up with anything, he turns his face toward us.

The three of us take in a breath all at once, stiffening in anticipation of what he is about to say to us as he opens his mouth to speak.

"Virginia." He says.

The three of us exchange a look. Sadie replies: "No, Hon… I'm Sadie and this—"

His eyes focus on Sadie, his eyes widening in surprise. "No, not you!" He says, then points a finger sharply to something behind us. *"Her!"*

We turn to look.

It's a duck; a white duck standing just behind us, facing the water.

He clarifies: "She's the leader. They all follow her around. But she's a good leader and doesn't take any bread until the rest of them have had some. I know bread is bad for them, and I know there's a sign saying not to bring any, but I do it anyway. They like it."

He focuses on the three of us again, then notices our empty hands. His eyebrows furrow together in what seems like aggravation. "You didn't bring any bread!" he says accusingly.

We pause for a beat, and he turns his attention back to the ducks, breaking off another crust to toss their way. I furrow my brow. *This* is Zeus?

"HUH?!" Tatum exclaims.

CHAPTER SIXTEEN

Sadie sits next to Zeus on his bench, and they take turns tossing bread to the ground while he talks. Tatum and I are close, far enough out of earshot so that we hear their voices but are unable to make out the specifics of what they're saying.

"Well," Tatum says, tossing a stick into the pond in front of us, "this is not what I expected when we started this little crusade today."

"What do you think's wrong with him?" I ask, glancing over my shoulder at Sadie and Zeus—my parents.

"My salon volunteers in nursing homes sometimes to give the old people in there some free, easy haircuts and some company, you know? The old people in them act just like that," Tatum juts her chin towards Zeus, "just not all there anymore. It's like they're having a conversation with someone else, and you're just a stand-in."

I sigh. "I can't imagine he'll be much help to us, then. What are the odds that Nyx doesn't have some dark and twisted ulterior motive for why she wants us to be fully back?"

Tatum looks at me, lids low, mouth in a straight line.

"I mean, we're all making a lot of assumptions about her. Tony doesn't seem to think anything is up."

"Of course not. Tony's a guy."

I roll my eyes and then turn and walk back to the bench. Tatum falls in step behind me.

He and Sadie are still tossing little balls of bread

to the ducks. Virginia the Duck waddles between Zeus and Sadie's feet, snatching the bread out of the air, so I guess everyone else has already gotten a turn.

Good grief, what am I saying?

Sadie is mid-sentence as we approach. "The reason we wanted to find you was that—"

"I'm not from here, you know." Zeus interrupts.

"Oh, yeah?" Sadie says, tilting her head to the side as she looks at him.

He nods. "I'm from Virginia. Not that one, but the other one." He points to Virginia the duck. "But I knew that the others would need me. Some are here. Some are… elsewhere. They don't know it yet, so I came here. I've been feeding the ducks while I wait."

"The others?" Tatum asks, "You mean the other gods?"

He looks at her and says, "Children need their father to show them how to tie their shoes. Change the oil. Feed the ducks." He frowns at Tatum and me. "Might be too late to change the oil."

"So, you came to teach us?" I ask him.

He fixes his gaze on me, sharp despite the rambling. "Only the ones who don't know. You can't teach a room full of experts. That's just boring."

Sadie presses on. "We were hoping you could tell us if we should drink the Nectar. Nyx wants us all to regain our immortality and rule over the mortals again. Do you know Nyx?"

The warmth drains from his face. His hands tighten around the bread. Then, without a word, he begins to shake his head slowly at first, but then gradually becomes more violent, like he's trying to shake a thought out of his skull. The ducks start to scatter away.

"Looks like he knows her," Tatum mutters.

Sadie lays a gentle hand on his shoulder. "It's okay, it's okay."

Zeus tops, glaring at her. "I'm here," he says, his voice dripping with bitterness, "I came, didn't I? I didn't want to come, but I did. I did what I was supposed to do.

Isn't that enough?"

Tatum and I exchange a glance.

"You didn't want to come?" Sadie asks.

Zeus rises. "There's a diner. They have my favorite pie. I have to go there now. I have to go."

I reach toward him, my fingertips grazing his arm. "Wait—"

He spins on me, voice booming: "I didn't want to come!"

A thunderclap cracks above in the clear, cloudless sky.

We all freeze.

His expression softens. "I'm sorry. I came because I knew I needed to. But I didn't want to. And now… I have to go get my pie."

He starts to leave, but after a few steps he pauses and looks back.

"I had a good life before, you know. I was a good

person. And then, I remembered everything. I remembered all the things I'd done. The ways I failed you. And… I don't want to be me anymore. I just want to feed the ducks. Eat my pie. Be home before the night comes." He hesitates. "I don't like the night. I don't like the dark."

And then he walks away.

"Here's what we know for sure," Tatum says, sitting sideways in the passenger seat so she can face both Sadie and me as we sit in the parking lot of the park, "Moros has already had his Nectar. Nyx probably has too. I don't know. Tulip *has* her Nectar."

"Do you know if Tony has summoned his Chrysantheion yet, Tulip?" Sadie asks, looking back at me.

I shrug.

"Very helpful," Tatum deadpans.

I glare at her, "But I know he's going to try. He was excited about being restored."

"Such. A. Guy." She shakes her head.

"What about you?" Sadie asks Tatum.

"Haven't tried. But, I guess if I do …" Tatum trails off, her lips pursing. "Being restored could be great for business—assuming there's no fine print on this deal."

"So, you're leaning towards yes?" Sadie presses.

"Maybe. Nyx lied about Zeus being back. We know that for sure now. And that's definitely shady. I didn't really understand what her whole goal could be before, but think about it—without Zeus in the picture, Nyx could take his old role as our leader. All the prayers that normally would have gone to him, they would now go to her!"

"That could have a whole lot of ramifications," Sadie replies with an edge of anxiety to her voice, "I don't know how much either of you remember about Nyx before—how strong she was…"

She trails off and looks between Tatum and me. We both shake our heads.

"There was always kind of a balance between all of us," Sadie explains, "how strong all of us used to be, I mean. The only exception, of course, was Zeus... and even *he* didn't mess with Nyx back then."

"Clearly, he's still not inclined to mess with her," Tatum says. "But maybe she was lying because she knew he was... like that? What are the odds Tulip was right and she really *just* wants us all back?"

"I only said that was possible," I argue.

"Right, and now *I'm* saying it's possible," Tatum replies sharply. "And if that's all it is... yeah. I'll take my Nectar."

"I don't plan on taking it," Sadie states flatly.

I look at her, genuinely shocked.

"Wait, what?" Tatum asks, apparently feeling the same way.

Sadie shrugs. "I love my life now. I have a wonderful husband, two beautiful girls, and a job I enjoy. I have everything I ever wanted. And it's enough."

Tatum scoffs, "And you, what, just forget about the rest of us and go back to your life before? Your literal daughter is sitting in the back seat right now!"

"Of course I wouldn't just go away out of your lives! Especially Tulip's! But divinity, immortality, and accepting offerings at altars for a good harvest? That isn't my life anymore. I faded from that life, and I'm happy with the new one I've made."

For the second time today, Sadie has left me feeling speechless. Nyx, Moros, and even Tony have had me thinking that drinking the Nectar and reclaiming our divinity wasn't just an opportunity; it was inevitable. Do we really have the option to say no?

Sadie drops Tatum off at her salon first. I move to the passenger seat when she's out of the car, having once again spent the entire ride mulling over Sadie's revelations to us.

"Penny for your thoughts," Sadie says playfully, after she's started heading towards my house.

"Are you really not going to take the Nectar?" I

ask quietly.

Sadie glances at me, eyes full of emotion. "I'm really not."

I look out my window and watch buildings zip by.

"What about you, Tulip?"

"What about me?"

"You've summoned your Nectar. Are you going to take it?"

I hesitate, my gaze fixed on the blur outside my window. "I don't know. I thought I was going to, but now… I don't know."

We sit in silence, the hum of the car filling the space. Then, the tires slow, crunching to a stop on the gravel shoulder of the road. I look over to see Sadie unbuckle and turn fully toward me.

"Tulip, I know that I haven't been in your life—*this* life—for very long. But I want you to know that meeting you again and having you in my life has been the best thing that has ever happened to me. Right up there with the birth of my girls."

Her voice is so steady and sure, all I can do is blink at her.

"I mean it, Hon. I am so thankful for whatever put us back together again. I love you. And I need you to know that, even if you drink your Nectar and reclaim your divinity, that will never change. I will never leave you. I will be here for you in whatever capacity you want."

My throat tightens. I turn back toward the window, blinking hard.

"And if you choose not to drink your Nectar, that will never change. You're stuck with me now, kid."

A single tear rolls down my cheek before I can stop it. I swipe it away quickly.

"Tulip, Honey. Look at me."

I draw in a shaky breath and turn my face back to her. Her eyes are suddenly glassy too. She takes my left hand in both of hers. They are warm, and her grip is firm.

"What is it that you *want*, Tulip?"

Another tear slips down my cheek, and this time I let it. I shake my head. "I don't know," I whisper.

She gives me a soft, sympathetic smile.

I take another shaky breath, trying to steady myself. "It feels like, no matter what I do, I'm going to let someone down."

"Like who?"

"If I take the Nectar, I feel like I'm turning my back on everything I've ever known for the last seventeen years. My friends, my mom... But if I don't then I'm letting down the gods. I'm letting down the mortals. I'm letting down Tony. I love him so much, and if I don't take the Nectar, I'm afraid of what that will mean for us."

"Why would it have to mean anything?"

"He wants it. His immortality. His kingdom back. If I don't take the Nectar, I can't be his queen anymore, can I? A mortal can't rule the Underworld. A mortal can't care for the dead."

Sadie nods slowly.

"But I just… my life before I awakened wasn't perfect, you know? It has been hard. *Really* hard. But it's also been so wonderful too."

"Tell me about it," Sadie says, smiling.

So, I do.

I tell her about my Friday night sleepovers with Val, and how we'd always watch horror movies. How Val knows me more than anyone else in my life ever has. I tell her how Val and I haven't spoken for over a month now. I tell her about how much I miss her. I tell her how afraid I've been to tell Val about me, about us.

I tell her about what life was like with both of my parents. How much fun we would have, just the three of us. I tell her about how my mom has changed, and how I want her to be happy, but also how disappointed I feel by the way my mom doesn't seem to understand anything about me anymore.

And then I ask her a question that has been haunting me since the night Nyx summoned all of us to meet—a question that I haven't even fully allowed myself to acknowledge: "Do you think that I could see my dad again if I take my Nectar?"

Sadie inhales sharply and looks out the windshield, then back at me. "I would like to say yes, Tulip. I think nothing would be more beautiful than that."

My heart sinks, already knowing the answer. "But?"

She holds my gaze. "Well, if you and Tony haven't been in the Underworld all this time... How could anyone else be there?

I feel myself deflating. I hadn't wanted to entertain that idea because I knew that this was probably the answer. But, hearing it confirmed still makes my chest tighten.

"Then where are they?" I ask, my voice coming out as a strangled whisper, "If they aren't in the

Underworld…"

Sadie sighs. "I don't know, Hon. But that doesn't mean you'll never see him again. We don't have all the answers yet."

Her answer doesn't solve anything, but her words make me feel as comforted as any answer can right now, so I hold onto them.

After giving my hand one final squeeze, she starts the car. She pulls back onto the road, and we ride the rest of the way home in silence.

When Sadie pulls the car up to my house, my stomach drops. Tony's car is waiting in the driveway.

"I'll text you later," I promise Sadie, unbuckling before she even gets the car to a full stop. I slam the door behind me and hurry toward Tony, who is already out of his car and storming toward me.

I open my mouth to speak, but Tony cuts me off as we meet in the middle of my driveway.

"Didn't need a ride today, huh?!" he exclaims, his hands thrown out wide. "Guess you didn't need your phone today either. Or have you just been ignoring me?"

His glare cuts past me to Sadie, who has parked and is watching with concern painted across her face.

"She was trying to reach me," I explain to him, "I didn't know—"

"What the hell, Persephone?!" Tony snaps.

The name makes my mouth sour. Persephone. Not Tulip. I close my eyes, suppressing the urge to roll them. I know it's my name, but it still feels wrong hearing it come out of his mouth.

I take a deep breath to steady myself. "I didn't—" but he cuts me off again.

"You've been avoiding me," he says accusingly, "all weekend, you barely spoke to me, you didn't see me, and now you skip school without saying anything, and I find you hanging out with *her.*" He cuts his eyes to Sadie again. "You've been acting strange ever since we saw Moros call his Chrysantheion, and you are going to tell me why right now!"

I feel my throat tighten and an icy-hot flush start

to rise on my face. "I'm trying to think, Tony!" I say in a shrill voice. "Sadie isn't going to call hers or drink the Nectar. It... it made me realize that we don't have to if we don't want to."

Tony's upper lip curls into a snarl of disgust. "Only a fool wouldn't want it."

"Zeus isn't taking it either," I tell him, "Oh yeah, we met him today. Turns out Nyx lied about him not being back. That doesn't strike you as a little odd?"

He rolls his eyes. "The only thing that does is prove my point," he says with venom, "my brother was never much of a leader anyway. What does it matter if we don't have *him* in our new era?"

I gape at him. In all the years I've known Tony, I've never heard him talk about anyone with so much dismissive disdain. I'm not even sure I ever heard Hades speak so hatefully in our old life.

Who even are *you anymore?* I think as I continue to look at him.

Tony takes a step back and looks down at the

ground, placing his hands on his hips. I watch as he takes a few calming breaths through his nose before he looks back up at me, his eyes much softer now.

"Look," he says in a low voice, stepping towards me and placing his hands on my biceps, bringing his forehead down to touch mine, and closing his eyes, "I just don't understand why you even need to think about this. Once we take the Nectar, we'll have everything we could ever dream of. The world will literally be ours, you and me, together. You... You'll be able to see your dad again." His eyes flutter open and bore into mine, our foreheads still touching. "You want that, don't you?"

My stomach twists. For a moment, I picture my dad's face again, as he looked back at me and laughed while we raced up the water slide steps. The ache of missing him roars up in my chest so strongly that I can hardly breathe. Suddenly, Tony's face in such proximity to mine feels suffocating. I jerk my head back, disconnecting us and look up at him.

I repeat Sadie's question: "If we haven't been in the Underworld all this time, how could anyone else be there now?"

His expression hardens again, and I see him glare in Sadie's direction once more. "I don't need to ask who put that in your head," he growls.

I say nothing, as I continue to stare up at him.

His gaze comes back to me, sharp and furious. "She just wants to keep you with herself, like always," he spits the words out venomously, "Demeter can never let go. She wants to keep you small. Mortal. She doesn't want to let you be who you really are."

"Tony, that's not true—"

"Stop calling me that!" he snaps, releasing my arms with a frustrated push.

"What?" I breathe, confused, "But that's you—"

"I'm not Tony anymore! I've never *been* Tony! I am more than that! Even when I didn't know it, I was always more than that!" His voice roars like thunder, and from behind me I hear Sadie opening her car door.

Throwing one final look of utter rage and disgust

at me, Tony turns and stomps back to his car. Without another word or a backwards glance, he flings the car door open and throws himself inside before slamming it shut. He turns the car on and tears out of my driveway, narrowly avoiding hitting Sadie as he swerves around her car in the road, the sound of screeching following him.

I stare after him. The sound of my pulse races in my ears. I don't realize until I run my hands over my face that they are shaking. Sadie is looking at me, and I can see even in my peripheral vision that her eyes are wide, and her hands are both raised to her mouth. I take a deep breath, trying to calm my nerves as the smell of burnt rubber floods my senses.

CHAPTER SEVENTEEN

I have never felt more alone.

Not when Mom has left me at home for late shifts. Not when the chasm opened up between me and Val. Not even after Dad died. But now? Now, the loneliness presses in from every side, suffocating me.

Yesterday, after Tony drove away in a rage and after I assured Sadie I would be okay, I went into my room and turned my phone back on. The screen flooded with missed calls and texts, so many at once that the phone froze. It didn't matter, though. I shoved it in the top drawer of my dresser. Out of sight, out of mind.

Now, as I drift from class to class in the final weeks of my senior year, I am swallowed whole by the laughter and chatter around me. Everyone belongs somewhere. Everyone belongs to someone. Everyone except me. I am the only one untethered. Even in the classes I share with my friends—well, former friends I guess—no one seems to notice me. I'm just a ghost.

Feeling like I might explode during my Spanish class, I ask the teacher to let me go to the restroom. He waves his hand dismissively in my direction, apparently too close to the end of the year to care where I go, or to respond out loud more than necessary. Instead of going to the restroom, I wander the halls aimlessly.

The sound of my shoes echoes on the laminate tiles as I climb up the stairs to the second floor of the building. It's really only the freshman classes up here, so I rarely have a reason to come this way. The doors along the long hallway are all shut, teachers either delivering lessons or taking their conferences behind them.

It's eerily quiet up here.

The doorways and rows of lockers that we aren't

allowed to use loom over me, watching me drift past. The sound of the fluorescent lights buzzes over my head and fills my senses. School isn't supposed to sound like this. There's supposed to be constant noise, signs of life. It's refreshing to break away from all the constant reminders of my loneliness, but at the same time, something about this level of silence around me is just as overwhelming. It sends a chill down my spine. I can't even hear voices muffled through the closed doors, or a distant cough from someone I can't see. The building feels abandoned.

The lights above me begin to flicker as I reach a point where this hall intersects with another, forming a perfect X. I slow my steps and look up. With a faint, sad little zap, they die. I glance behind me and see that the whole hall I just walked through is darkened. I turn back to face front to find that the only source of light is a window at the far end of the corridor ahead of me like the light at the end of a tunnel. Otherwise, the hall is shrouded in a blue shadow, and the steady buzz from above has also died. The silence is absolute.

"Strange place to find yourself. Lost your way?"

The voice comes from behind me. I jolt, heart leaping into my throat as I whirl around.

A woman with golden skin leans against the corner of the intersection, one foot casually propped against it. Her hands are folded across her chest. She's wearing the uniform of the school security officers, but I'm pretty sure I've never seen her before. Her hair, which I'm pretty sure is supposed to be pulled back, hangs loose on her shoulders. It looks dark brown, but the distant light from the window catches on something in it. Strands of silver, shimmering in the light. They look like shooting stars traveling down her hair.

Though a small smile tugs at the corners of her lips, her eyes watch me with unnerving intensity. They don't look wrong, exactly. But they seem too sharp somehow. Too steady. It feels like she's doing more than looking at me. She's looking *in* me. For a second, I swear they flash. But then I blink and assume it must have just been a trick of the distant light.

On her utility belt, I spot a large ring of keys.

228

They don't look like the keys I've seen the teachers and other security officers around here use before. They look bigger. Grander. Oddly ornate with big teeth and designs along the length.

She tilts her head to the side as though studying me, and I see a shiny necklace under the casually unbuttoned collar of her otherwise crisp uniform with three dangling charms on it: a torch, a dagger, and something else... a dog, maybe? Or maybe it's a wolf, its muzzle lifted into a silent howl.

"Um..." I realize I've been studying her for a weird amount of time. "My teacher said I could go to the bathroom."

"Seems to me like you've found yourself in a yellow wood." The officer replied, apparently ignoring my excuse for being here.

I raise one eyebrow. "Huh?"

Her smile widens in amusement. "Like the poem," she chuckles, "you ever heard it? *The Road Not Taken.*"

I shake my head slowly.

"That's a shame. It's one of my favorites. 'Two roads diverged in a yellow wood, and sorry I could not travel both, and be one traveler, long I stood.'"

"Oh, yeah. That's pretty," I say, trying to appease her.

"What do you think is the better option? The road that's more worn down, a path formed... The kind of road that has practically been chosen for you? Or the road that's still green? The road that so few people have traveled down that you have to make your own path on it?"

I blink at her, trying to process the question. "I... I don't know."

She nods. "Both options have their strengths. There's certainly a kind of security in choosing the first road. A kind of safety. You have access to guidance; there are fewer risks involved. On the other hand, there's something so exciting about carving out one's own path, isn't there? Forging your own way can make you stronger."

I sigh. "It sounds harder, though."

Chuckling, she replies, "Absolutely. More obstacles, more struggles, and fewer guidelines. You will probably feel like you have no idea what you're doing more often than not if you choose *that* path. But there's beauty in the struggle, too. The second road might be hard, but it teaches you to see things differently."

I say nothing, but look off to the side, staring into the distance as I mull over her words.

Out of the corner of my eye, I see her rise from the wall and step towards me, slowly closing the distance between us. As she takes each agonizingly slow step, she recites: "Two roads diverged in a wood, and I—I took the one less traveled by, and that has made all the difference."

She is right next to me, so close that I feel the heat of her body and smell the faint scent of lavender coming off her. The air around her prickles and, as it touches me, creates a tickle on the back of my head and neck. Without warning, she reaches a hand towards me and strokes a stray lock of hair behind my ear. The touch is feather-light, but my skin flares hot under it, every hair on my arms standing at attention.

Startled by her touch, I jerk away and turn to look at her, only to find that I am alone in the hall again.

Above me, the lights flicker back on with a buzz.

CHAPTER EIGHTEEN

When I get home from school, after enduring a tense and silent car ride with my mom, I toss my backpack into my room and go straight to the backyard.

Rather than go into the greenhouse right away, I stomp to the edge of the yard, where our property line meets the vast field of grass, and plop onto the ground looking out to the field, my legs bent and arms resting on my knees. I hunch my shoulders forward a little into a slump and let my eyes flutter closed. I try to forget the fact that the Chrysantheion is just a few steps away.

A slight breeze stirs the grass. At the sound of the

blades moving in sync, I open my eyes and gaze out into the field. I let my eyes drift across the horizon of tall grass dancing towards the clear sky. Without warning, a tickle at the back of my head pulls me into a memory.

I stood in a scorched, blackened field with a mortal woman. An apothecary... One of the few women who were still practicing then. I was disguised as a mortal woman myself.

She looked at me, hopeless.

"I'm ruined!" She cried in our ancient tongue.

She had spent years delivering babies safely in her Kome. She healed countless sick, tended countless hearts. She used herbs and flowers from her own field to make her own balms and potions—medicines that people desperately needed. I saw all of it as I reached out and touched her shoulder. I saw her heart, and how it longed only to help her people.

With one hand still on her shoulder as she buried her face in her hands, I looked out to the wasteland around us. Destroyed by a fire that many had tried in vain to stop, this field was the only one for miles that grew what she needed.

As she cried, I swept my other hand in front of me in a grand gesture, palm down to the earth, and called forth the blooms that had been so violently demolished. Vines of vibrant and lush green, vivid reds and whites, all burst forth from the dry earth, splitting the ruined soil and stretching skyward. The soil beneath the charred surface surged upward, overtaking the ruined parts of itself like ocean waves crashing over sand.

In seconds, not only was her field restored—it was improved. Never again would fires be able to overtake it. Never again would this healer suffer such devastation from any element. She would be able to heal her people for decades to come.

The fragrance of new life washed over the mortal woman. She raised her face from her hands. I removed my hand from her shoulder. She gaped around her in awe and turned to me.

"You've tended to so many," I said to her gently, "Now, no flame, no storm, no winter will be able to

235

touch what you have earned."

With a gasp, I am brought out of my memory and back to the edge of the grass field.

I jump to my feet and gape at the field of grass before me. I once restored an entire field of ruined, burned life with just a sweep of my hand. I glance down at my palms and then back out to the grass in front of me.

I adjust my feet to steady myself where I stand. I close my eyes and breathe in, deep. I extend my hands out in front of me, palms down. Just as I've done so many times in the greenhouse, just as I did in the memory, I call flowers forth from the earth—poppies, lilies, irises, tulips. I will them to pull up and out of the ground and stretch higher than any of the tall grass. I imagine the field covered in bright, brilliant colors. My heart burns and aches with the effort. I push myself until I can no longer bear the weight and the strain.

I drop to my knees, feeling like my heart just got done playing tug of war with a brick wall. I take a few gulps of air and then open my eyes.

236

Grass. As far as the eye can see, it is still just grass.

I slouch forward, letting my head roll down. On the ground, just in front of my knees, is one single poppy.

Letting out a frustrated growl, I rise. I want to storm into the greenhouse but am still so weak from the wasted effort that all I can manage is a weak shuffle.

The air inside is warm and humming. The plants all turn their attention to me, and I pause to breathe in their crisp, wet scent. Then, I kneel at the back shelf, fingers fumbling over cool metal and rough plastic until I find what I came for.

The Chrysantheion glows as dazzlingly as the day it first bloomed, its petals glimmering as if lit from within. It shows no sign of wilting. It looks like nothing else in here. It looks like a god among mortals.

The thought makes me let out a bitter snort.

Nectar pools within the heart of the flower, its sweet scent spiraling through the air around it. It makes my stomach twist. I am almost repulsed by the strength of my body's desire to raise it to my lips and drink.

I lift the pot into my lap and sit cross-legged on the ground, staring into the liquid, completely transfixed.

Tony's voice echoes in my head.

The world will literally be ours. You and me, together... You'll be able to see your dad again.

Then, Sadie's voice. It echoes through just as loud as Tony's but steadier. Calmer.

I have everything I ever wanted. And it's enough... I faded from that life, and I'm happy with the new one I've made.

"Two roads diverged in a wood." I whisper to myself, remembering the security officer's—or whoever she was—words.

What is it you want, *Tulip?* Sadie had asked me just yesterday. Months ago, I didn't have an answer or even the illusion of options. Now, it seems that I have nothing but options, all the freedom of a god, and the answer to that question feels further out of my reach than ever before.

Sadie built a life with people she loves because she knew what she wanted. If I refuse the Nectar, what would I build? What would I even want?

Tony knows what he wants. If I choose his path, my destiny is handed to me on a silver platter. No questions. No sweat.

Thousands of years separate my old life from this one, and still I am pulled between two versions of myself, and the two people who love the version that they get. Some things never change.

The Nectar swirls like a supernova. It would be so easy. Just lift the flower to my lips and drink. Only a few inches of air between me and immortality. Between me and divinity. Between me and destiny.

But would it be enough?

I think of Tony. I've known him for most of my life. I loved him even before we remembered we were husband and wife. King and Queen. But would that be the case if we hadn't awakened? Would I have loved him *this* way if he were still simply Tony? Would he have chosen me if I were only Tulip?

I remember the way he held me at my dad's funeral. I remember how he'd always made sure I got to sit next to him at every one of his birthday parties when we were little. Once, a bigger kid accidentally tripped me on the playground in third grade, and Tony ran after him and made him apologize to me. I smile at the memory.

Yes. He loved me even before we awakened. Even when he was Tony, and not Hades. He loved me fiercely.

I feel my fingers tighten around the flowerpot.

Just inches of air…

I raise the pot. The sweet, warm scent of the Nectar washes over my face. I close my eyes and breathe it in, the energy from the Chrysantheion practically vibrating my palms.

I open my eyes and see my face reflected in the sparkling surface of the Nectar. My eyes are wide with desire. I don't even recognize my reflection. The sight makes me gasp and I lower the pot again to get the image away from me. The Nectar gleams, a pulse of light in the shadows. I swear the flower leans toward me, as if it can sense how close I just came to surrendering to it.

Heart hammering, I put it back in its hiding place on the bottom shelf and move the gardening supplies back in front of it. I need more time. I am not ready to choose one way or another yet, no matter how tempted I was just now.

With dragging feet, I leave the greenhouse and trudge back to the house. Every step away from the Chrysantheion seems to weaken its pull on me, but only barely. As I approach the back of the house, I make a concentrated effort to shove it out of my thoughts, at least for right now. When I slide open the back door, I notice Mom sitting at the kitchen table, her face turned towards the window that looks out into the backyard. She stares blankly into it, her hands clasped together under her chin.

I pause at the door. I consider saying nothing and making a beeline for my room, but instead, I slowly step toward the kitchen table and sit across from her. I stare at her. She continues to stare out into the backyard.

I almost think she doesn't realize I'm here until she speaks.

"You and your dad loved being out there," she says, "I wish I loved it as much as you two."

I look out the window too and see the greenhouse. I don't know what to say. After days of us not talking about anything, this seems like an odd way for her to open a conversation. I brace myself for whatever she might say next.

"I was always so jealous of the bond you two had," Mom continues, "he was such a good parent. I had always wanted to be a mom, you know. I was ready to start having babies before the ink on our marriage certificate was dry. When I found out I was pregnant with you, I could have exploded with happiness."

She glances at me, a small smile on her lips and a dreamy, faraway look in her eyes. Then with a soft, barely audible chuckle, she turns her face back to the window.

"I was ready to be your mom up until they put you in my arms at the hospital. Then, suddenly, I was terrified out of my mind. I didn't know what to do. I didn't know how to feel connected to you anymore. When you were an actual part of me, it was so easy... But suddenly, here I was with an entire human being that needed me, who I had waited for all this time, who I had been so excited to meet, and it was like... Like I didn't recognize you."

I feel my shoulders sink. I didn't know any of this about how my mom felt after I was born. I assumed that Mom felt the same way about me that all the moms in all the movies seem to—overcome with joy and instantly in love with their new babies. I guess that's an ignorant assumption to make, but neither she nor my dad ever gave me any reason to think differently.

"It wasn't like that for your dad, though," she

continues, "it was the opposite, actually. He seemed so nervous throughout the whole pregnancy. Anxious to make sure we were bringing you home to the perfect setting. He worried that he wouldn't be able to bond with you, because a book for expecting dads said that was typical for the father experience or something." She rolls her eyes. "But the second he saw you… You had him wrapped around your little finger. He was smitten from the first second he held you. I hardly had to do anything apart from feeding you, because he *wanted* to take care of you. I knew he'd be a good dad, but he went so far above and beyond my already-high expectations. And I was so jealous of how easy it seemed to be for him to feel so… connected to you. It made me hate him a little bit for the first couple of months of your life."

I jerk my head back in surprise. She turns her head towards me again.

"I didn't really hate him. I just mean that's how intensely jealous I felt of the bond he had with you. It all seemed to just come so naturally for him; it was like he was made to be your dad. It never felt like it came naturally to me."

She drops her hands and starts tracing patterns on the wood of the kitchen table with her fingertips, watching the movements intently.

"Your grandma was no help, either. Any time I tried talking to her about how hard it was, and how much I was struggling, she would just remind me that I wanted to be a mother, and I had to take the bad with the good. Women in her generation didn't complain about that kind of thing. They just took a *fake it 'til you make it* attitude, and I think she expected me to do that. Not super helpful, but I think she meant well. Anyway… Your dad encouraged me to go to therapy. Not in a mean way. He just knew I needed help, and he didn't know how to help me himself. That's how I figured out that I had postpartum."

She sighs, closes her eyes, and her hands stop tracing.

"Eventually, I started to get better. It didn't happen overnight, of course. But… Slowly, I started feeling like I could do it. Like I could be a decent mom to you." Opening her eyes, she smiles and continues: "Do you remember your twelfth birthday?"

I nod. "My surprise party."

The year I turned twelve, Dad had taken me to the mall one day to make a stuffed animal. I had picked out a soft bunny and Dad even let me pick out a scent to put in it. I was allowed to get all the clothes and accessories I wanted for it. I turned the simple bunny into a full glam rock star, at least in my opinion. It was covered in sequins and tulle with a little plastic microphone and shiny shoes. It had already been one of the best birthday gifts I had ever received.

But then, when we arrived home to the darkened house, as soon as I flipped the lights on, all my friends jumped out from behind walls and furniture and shouted "SURPRISE!" in unison. My mom walked out with a massive double chocolate cake, decorated intricately with chocolate flowers. Everyone sang to me. We played games that Mom facilitated. We all watched my favorite movie, gathered around the living room TV. We ate pizza, ice cream, and the most delicious, beautiful cake I had ever seen. It was perfect. That was the most love I had ever felt in one room at that point in my life, and it was all for me.

"I had been planning that surprise party for months. Your dad helped, of course, but it was important to me that I did most of it. And then, I pulled it off. You came in, and I had never seen you so happy in your whole life. Seeing your smile that day… That was the moment I felt like I was maybe turning into a good mom."

"You *are* a good mom. You've always been a good mom." I tell her desperately, my voice coming out thin and cracked.

She shakes her head. "Well, if I am, it's only because of your dad."

I stare at her. All this time, I've been so focused on how Dad's death has impacted me. Even when I think of the ways Mom has changed since he died, it's had nothing to do with her, but rather how the changes in her have affected my life. How she hasn't noticed me, the changes I've been going through, how she doesn't laugh anymore and how uncomfortable and sad that makes me.

The realization feels like a weight so heavy that it could bury me into the ground right now, and I feel so ashamed that I'd welcome it.

"He always seemed to know how to fix everything. How to take care of everything. He was my rock, Tulip." She looks me in the eyes, her own glistening with tears. "I haven't known how to... how to be without him. I expected to grow old with him. I expected to travel the world with him after you were out of the house, to be the fun grandparents to your kids with him."

Her voice cracks at the last word. A tear runs down her cheek. I feel my throat tighten and my eyes burn. I have to look away from her and towards the window to keep myself from breaking down in front of her right now. When she speaks again, her voice is thick with raw emotions.

"I haven't been what you need me to be. It's like when you were a newborn all over again. I have felt like I don't know how to get myself through this, let alone get *you* through this. And I am so, so sorry, baby."

I close my eyes, but not before tears spill out of them and drip from my jaw. I hear Mom's chair scrape against the floor, and her footsteps approach. Then, I feel her arms wrap around me and her head rest on top of mine.

I let out a sob, then turn to bury my face into my mom's shoulder. She strokes my hair and gently rocks me back and forth. I smell our fabric softener in her clothes. It wraps me up in familiarity. I feel her sobs through her chest as she tightens her arms around me. I realize how deeply I've missed her. My shame and my sorrow overwhelm me. I want to apologize to my mom for being so self-absorbed all this time.

It was once my responsibility to take care of people just like my mom and my dad, and for months now, I have been carrying so much sadness and resentment towards my mom for not seeing me… But I hadn't been seeing *her*. If I can't even see my own mother through her grief, how will I ever even be able to think I can guide mortals through theirs?

As she holds me, I hear her whispering either to me or to herself: "We're going to get through this. We're going to get through this."

I cling to her, both of us tightening our arms around one another. But beneath the warmth of her arms and this moment, I can still feel the pulse of the Chrysantheion in my fingers, and it whispers its own promises to me too.

CHAPTER NINETEEN

The house is so quiet I can hear crickets through my window.

Though Mom went to bed hours ago, I lay awake, staring up at the ceiling, my chest still throbbing from the conversation and the cry with her earlier. For the first time since Dad died, as I curl my hands around the top of my blanket, I feel actual hope. Hope that things are going to be okay. Hope that I might have my mother back after all this time, or at least that I may get her back eventually.

But I feel something else too, beneath all this

hope—the sharp pain of my distance from Val, gnawing at me, even louder now in the quiet.

A month ago, I would have texted her immediately to tell her about the talk with Mom. Not having her to tell everything to feels completely unnatural to me, like when I got my braces taken off in eighth grade and my tongue kept searching for the brackets on my too-smooth teeth for days afterwards.

Sitting up in bed, I realize something: I can't choose whether to regain my divinity and immortality without at least trying to make things right with her first. Since we met, Val has always been more than my best friend; she has been my compass, the one person I could consistently depend on for advice and direction. In all my uncertain times, Val has been there to offer her insight in a completely honest, though not unkind, way. There has never been anything I couldn't tell her that she didn't eventually understand. She is my person and always has been.

I need to tell her everything.

God, I wish she were here now. My heart

clenches in my chest. She may think I'm crazy. She might laugh in my face or, worse, tell me to never speak to her again. But I have to try. I have to tell her about my awakening. About my past life. About Tony, about Sadie, about Nyx and her plan, and about my Chrysantheion.

The thought of the flower hidden in my greenhouse sends a chill through my body, and an unbearable ache to go out there and take it. It calls to me, so persistently that I can feel its pull beneath my skin like a second pulse. I can practically feel the vibrations of it thrumming in my palms.

I can't give in to it—not yet at least. First, I have to talk to Val.

But as I get out of bed and slip on my shoes, I think *maybe it won't hurt to see it. Just one more time before I decide. Just for a moment.*

I glide through the house as if on autopilot, slowly sliding the back door shut behind me. As I walk across the yard towards the greenhouse, an ache coils in my stomach, urging me to run. The muscles in my legs involuntarily twitch and my heart sputters in my chest with the instinct to sprint. Somehow, I resist, but every step forward intensifies that ache, my impatience boiling deep within me.

It feels like I blink and am immediately crouched on the ground in the greenhouse again, clutching the pot in my sweaty palms and letting the warm light of the Nectar wash over my face.

My thoughts flicker to Val, once again wishing she were here. If she saw this, if she touched it and felt as drawn to it as I do, then maybe I could know I'm not imagining the weight of its pull. Being here alone with it, without anyone or anything to anchor me, makes me feel certain that the power of the Nectar is going to swallow me whole.

The thought intensifies inside me, tightening my heart like a desperate prayer: *I wish Val were here.*

The Chrysantheion vibrates in my hands and the glow of the Nectar pulses like a heartbeat, syncing with my own. The inside of my head fills with soft buzzing, like there are honeybees all around me. I don't even realize that I've raised the Chrysantheion closer to my face until I see it reflected at me in the surface of the Nectar for the second time today.

And then, I whip my head around when I hear a sound. A thump outside. The shutting of a car door.

My stomach drops, and I feel the color drain from my face. I freeze. I've woken Mom up. I'm caught.

A shadow falls across the greenhouse door, plunging me into total darkness. The doorknob twists slowly, the door creaking open cautiously. The warmth of this person's presence brushes against me before I even see who it is.

I blink, dumbfounded at the familiar face I see peeking in.

"Tulip?" Val whispers, her voice thick with sleep, as if she's just woken up. She looks disheveled, like she's sleepwalking... Like something drew her here without her knowing why.

Then, her brow furrows and her eyes widen in confusion as her gaze falls to the glowing flower in my hands.

"Val," I gasp.

At the sound of her name, Val blinks rapidly and looks at my face, then at her surroundings, as if just now noticing that she isn't at home in bed.

"What's going on?" She asks, a panicked edge to her voice.

My gaze falls back to the Chrysantheion. Just a second ago, as I held it and wished desperately for Val to be here, the glow of the Nectar changed and seemed to pulse in time with my heartbeat. And now, here she is. After a month of silence, Val is in my greenhouse, in the middle of the night, looking like she just woke up.

Did the Chrysantheion summon her here? Did I?

I let out a shaky breath and peel my eyes away from the glowing flower to turn back to Val. I rise to my feet, step toward her, and see her eyes once again dart to it, narrowing in suspicion.

"Val," I say, drawing her gaze back to my face, "There's, umm… There are some things I want to tell you… I want to tell you everything."

"And now, I have this flower. If I drink the Nectar inside it, I'll have all my powers back. I'll be immortal like I was before. Nyx wants all of us to come together again in a couple of days and do it."

We sit cross-legged across from one another on the floor of the greenhouse. The Chrysantheion in its pot sits next to me. The whole time I talked, Val's focus kept jumping back and forth between me and it, like she wanted to keep an eye on it to make sure it was truly there, and not a mirage. Now, though, she has her full attention on me.

I let out a breath, finally having gotten everything that I wanted to say—which really was *everything*—out.

Val's face is completely blank. She did not say a single word to me while I unleashed everything I had been holding back, her mouth a flat line. She stares at me, unblinking, for several seconds.

I squirm under her stare.

"What?!" She finally exclaims, slamming her palms down on the ground and furrowing her brow at me. "You really expect me to buy all that?! That you're an ancient goddess with magical powers, that Tony's like the Grim Reaper or something?"

"Well, actually—"

"And that's why you've been acting so weird? Do you think I'm stupid, Tulip? What are you, *nuts*?!"

She rises to her feet, and I grab the Chrysantheion and rise to mine, terrified that she's about to storm out.

"Val, wait! How else would you explain this?" I ask desperately, holding the flowerpot out towards her as evidence.

She pauses and eyes the flower suspiciously again with her head slightly turned away, like she's afraid to look at it fully. Still, she stays in place and side-eyes it for a minute, and I can see the wheels in her head turning as she considers all she's heard.

Eventually, she looks at my face again, crossing

her arms, and says, "Okay. Prove it, then."

I jerk my head back in surprise. "Prove it?" I ask, "Prove *what*?"

"You're the goddess, Tulip. Goddess of Spring, right? So, prove it." She turns her full body towards me now, challenging me.

I look around the greenhouse awkwardly. I could summon a new plant, give new life to show her I'm telling the truth… But I'm holding my last unoccupied flower pot.

My eyes drift across the sea of greenery lining each shelf, eventually landing on the Boston Fern. Once near-death, I had rehabilitated it even before awakening. Since that had happened, and I started exercising my powers over plants again, it has thrived.

Still, it remains on the smaller side.

That's it.

Placing the Chrysantheion down on the ground in a corner where I won't run the risk of knocking it over with my clumsy feet, I reach for the fern and hold it in front of me so Val can see it.

"Okay," I breathe, "watch this."

After making sure she is indeed watching, I focus all my attention on the fern. I take a deep breath in through my nose, then blow it out slowly through my mouth. I picture exactly what I want to happen in my mind and then bring my focus to my heart. From it, I pull what I want from the fern, as if it's tied to a rope.

Val's eyes widen as, in my hands, the fronds of the fern expand, like they've been cramped up and are finally being allowed to stretch out. New leaves unfurl like palms opening to the sky. The fern gets so big that it completely blocks my view of Val. I have to adjust my hands so that I hold it from beneath, so I don't drop it. Then, eventually, I have to set it on the ground.

I stop only when the fern threatens to burst the pot it is in.

I hesitantly raise my gaze to meet Val's, but she is still staring at the fern. Her eyes are so wide that it looks like they might roll out of the sockets at any second. Her mouth hangs open, her lower jaw completely slack, and she is breathing in short, fast, raspy gasps.

I step around the fern and reach out a hand towards her.

"Val?" I say.

At her name, her eyes snap back to mine and she smacks my hand away.

"OH MY GOD!" She exclaims and begins pacing to her left.

"Oh my god?!" she says after two steps. She turns and starts toward her right, realizing she is out of room to the left.

"Oh my *god!*" she repeats, coming to a complete halt after three steps in her new direction and turning on her heel towards me, her brow furrowed and her eyes blazing in anger.

Then, she sighs. Her face relaxes. Her eyes soften as she stares into mine. She raises her hands and digs her fingers into her hair, balling them into fists. Something she has done when stressed for as long as I've known her.

"Oh... my god..." And with that final word, she lowers herself down to the floor. Her arms drop limply to her sides with a smacking sound as her hands hit the ground. She is no longer looking at me, or at the fern. Her eyes have a distant, almost glazed look.

I wait a few seconds before I slowly lower myself to the ground in front of her. Cautiously, I once again reach out towards her and, thankfully, this time she doesn't slap it away. I place it on her shoulder.

"I know this is... A lot," I say, "but now you know why I've been so..." my voice trails off.

Val becomes present again, narrowing her eyes at me ever so slightly.

"You really think this excuses everything, Tulip?" she hisses, "Okay, fine. You're an ancient goddess reincarnated. Okay, you can make plants with your mind or whatever. What does any of that have to do with you being such a shitty friend? How did it make you shut me out? *Me?*"

I drop my hand. A lump rises in my throat. I try to swallow it, but it won't budge. I lower my gaze to my lap as I feel my chest tighten.

"It doesn't," I mutter. Then, I raise my eyes to hers. "I'm sorry, Val. I'm *so* sorry. I have been a really bad friend, to you and to everyone else. I shut you out, and all you ever tried to do was be there for me, support me. You didn't deserve that. I know it doesn't make up for anything I've done, but I am really, really sorry. If you can't forgive me, I understand... But I hope that you will, in time."

The lump in my throat has turned painful, and I feel the back of my eyes burning with tears. I don't want to cry, but I worry that there's nothing I can do to stop it.

Val stares at me for what feels like forever, her own eyes getting glassy. Finally, she begins to nod slowly, then rubs the back of her hand over her eyes. She smacks her tongue against the roof of her mouth, inhales quickly then, in a perfectly even tone, says: "Well, okay then."

I blink rapidly at her. "Okay, then?" I ask.

"Yep. We're good." She says, looking at me stone-faced for a second before a smile creeps up the corners of her lips. She lets out a laugh like she can't hold it in. "You don't seriously think I had it in me to stay mad at you, did you? The last month has been more than enough."

My jaw drops. "So... Just like that, you forgive me?!"

"Heck yeah, chica," she says, waving her hand breezily, "I mean, you're not *just* my best friend. You're the effing goddess of Spring! What, am I just *not* gonna forgive you? Please." She rolls her eyes playfully.

I let out a quick bark of a laugh in pure relief. I feel tingling all over my body, like the blood is rushing back to all my major limbs. I let out a shaky breath, suddenly feeling lightheaded.

"So," Val says, clapping her hands together, ready to get down to business, "tell me more about this special, glowy, magical flower juice, and let's make ourselves a good, old-fashioned pros and cons list."

CHAPTER TWENTY

Val drives me to school after sleeping over. We had to make a stop by her house so she could change, which we decided called for a coffee run. We wouldn't have been able to make it to school in the first place without some caffeine, having spent all night talking in the greenhouse.

By the time we make it to school, we are deliriously giggly from the lack of sleep and the espresso shots in our iced coffees. We breeze through the morning like we're walking on air, all things right in each of our worlds now that we are once again connected at the hip.

I feel lighter than I have in weeks.

At lunch, though I see our group exchange looks briefly as we approach the table together, no one mentions the sudden return of me to the table when they see that things between Val and me are as they used to be—how they should have been all along.

At the sound of the bell ending our shared lunch period, my friends and I rise from the table and head in different directions. I am pushing in my chair when out of the corner of my eye, I see a dark figure standing perfectly still in the chaos of the hallway cramped with moving bodies. I look up and my stomach clenches.

At the end of the hallway to my right—the hallway that happens to be the route I usually take to my class right after lunch—is Tony, standing frozen, and staring at me. My heart flutters at the sight of him, but then I take in his expression and feel the color drain from my cheeks.

His face is completely blank. He stares at me, unblinking, offering me nothing, not even the faintest hint of what he feels. I blink and then suddenly, it's not

267

Tony I'm looking at anymore. It's Hades, still standing like a statue at the end of the hall, still wearing Tony's red Adidas hoodie over Tony's black pants, and Tony's red sneakers. But it is unmistakably Hades, tall and imposing, exactly as he was all those centuries ago, as he ruled over the underworld.

The familiar tickle is at the back of my head, and I get flashes of memories in my mind's eye, too quick to catch, but all of *him*. My legs wobble. My lungs burn. I try to move, but my body will not obey me. My breaths are shallow and fast. My ears fill with cotton and all the sounds of the cafeteria fade and morph into a piercing ring.

All I can do is stare back at him as everyone moves around us, like minnows in a pond. No one sees him. How can no one see him?

I feel a hand on my arm.

"You okay?" Val's voice cuts through the ringing, abruptly bringing me back to myself with a jolt.

I jump and snap my attention to her. Her eyes are

wide with concern. Our other friends are gone. The cafeteria is almost empty.

Panting, I look back to where Hades was and see that he is gone. The hallway, too, is much emptier than it was just a second ago.

"Yeah," I breathe, hand over my heart, "sorry, I… I don't know what that was."

She grins at me, trying her best to be reassuring even though I can still see worry in her eyes.

I let out a slow, grounding breath. "Come on, we don't need to make a habit of being late this close to graduation."

I link my arm with hers and we make our way to class. All the while, I fight the urge to look over my shoulder every few steps.

As Val drives me home from school, we shout-sing Chappell Roan songs. Tony wasn't in Chemistry at the end of the school day, and I have been avoiding thoughts of him. We haven't spoken since our fight on Monday—the longest we've gone without talking since we both awakened. Tomorrow is the night Nyx expects all of us to meet again and reclaim our divinity. Is he really planning on punishing my hesitation and doubt with the silent treatment until then?

As Val's car crests the hill on my street and we get a clear view of my house, my question is answered.

"Was Tony at school today? How did he beat us to your house?" Val asks, lowering the volume on her car's radio.

"I didn't see him," I reply. His car sits in my driveway, but I don't see him in it. Under my breath, I mutter: "What is he doing here?"

Val pulls into the driveway, behind Tony's car, and puts the car into park. Mom isn't home yet.

"Want me to come with you?" She asks, starting to reach for the keys.

"No, it's okay. I probably need to talk with him." I say, though after this afternoon, I want to scream and beg Val not to leave me alone.

What's the matter with you? This is Tony! Your Tony. Every version of you loves him.

"Okay," Val says in a cheerful tone. "I need to pick our movie for tomorrow night's sleepover, anyway! Assuming you'll have time after your big god-meeting. Do you think you will?"

"Umm, I'm not sure how it's all going to go down. I'll probably come home with you after school but then sneak out at showtime. Is that okay?"

"Of course! You feeling any closer to a decision?"

I sigh.

She reaches out and squeezes my hand. "I'm with you, no matter what."

I smile at her. "Thank you," I say, then unbuckle and get out of the car. "See you tomorrow."

After I shut the passenger door, Val drives off. I turn my attention back to Tony's empty car. I glance toward the front door and see that he isn't there. Somehow, I know that if I go around the house to the

271

backyard, I will find him in the greenhouse.

I lean my backpack against the garage and make my way around to the back.

As I approach the greenhouse and reach for the door, a golden glow bleeds through the glass. I squint as the light refracts through the glass, annoyed at the sun's sudden appearance.

But then I stop dead in my tracks. Even my heart seems to stop for a beat. I realize in an instant that this glow isn't from the sun. It's too steady, too alive, and it's coming from *within* the greenhouse. I don't need to open the door to know what he's found.

I do open the door though, because I know I have to face this.

Tony's back is to me. Something in his stance is different—wrong. He turns toward slowly, my flowerpot in his hands, and I take him in.

He has always favored bright colors, but now he is dressed all in black. He is wearing a crisp, black, short-sleeved collared shirt, unbuttoned all the way with a black T-shirt underneath it, over black pants and black shoes. He has never worn rings for as long as I've known him, but today he has two silver bands on his right hand and one on his left. He even seems to be standing up straighter than usual.

As I look at him, I realize that there is very little of *my* Tony left. He is more Hades now. *My* Hades?

"Seph," he breathes, eyes gleaming, "you did it!"

I shut the greenhouse door behind me and look at him. "Yeah, I guess I did."

His smile widens and a small laugh escapes him, like he cannot contain it. He puts the flowerpot down on a shelf near him, then rushes towards me, sweeping me up into his arms and spinning me around.

When he sets me down, he grabs my face and crushes his lips against mine. The force knocks the air out of me.

I wrench back, gulping air. He is still grinning as I look up at him, his eyes still wide in a way that makes me squirm.

273

"I figured out how to summon mine, too!" he exclaims. He lifts the flowerpot, turning it at eye level. "I'm saving it for tomorrow, when we all meet. I knew you'd come around."

I say nothing, too overstimulated by his excitement to know what to say.

He doesn't notice my silence, and keeps rotating the flowerpot, muttering, "That's crazy. *Crazy.*"

After letting him examine it for several minutes, I say, "Do you think you could put it back on the shelf where I had it? I don't want Mom to find it if she comes out here."

"Yeah, sure," he says without looking at me. After another second or two of looking at it, he finally crouches low to put the Chrysantheion back in its hiding place.

I stand awkwardly, shifting my weight from one foot to the other as he rises and looks back toward me, smiling. I try to force a smile to my lips, but it feels more strained, like a grimace.

Around me, my plants make tiny side-to-side movements, like they are trembling.

His smile falters, and he furrows his brow and narrows his eyes at me like he's just now seeing me.

I fidget under his gaze, and I can't maintain eye contact with him.

"You just got here…" he says slowly, "but the Chrysantheion was already here. Hidden…"

My heart is racing so furiously in my chest that it hurts. I feel like it's going to leap up my throat at any second and take off running. The plants' trembling grows more violent. I try desperately to meet his eyes, but they are staring so intently into mine that I flinch away almost as soon as I look at him.

He takes a slow breath in. "Persephone," he says in a low, controlled voice, like he is fighting to remain composed, "how long has it been since you summoned it?"

My gaze falls to my feet as I feel heat rise in my cheeks. "Since Monday."

I risk looking up at him to see his expression darkening. The tickle at the back of my head brings with it another flash, another fleeting memory—wailing sobs in the distance and a pair of cold, unfeeling black eyes. The image vanishes from my mind almost as soon as it appears, slipping through my fingers like smoke.

He takes a step towards me. Every urge inside my body screams for me to step back, to keep the space between us. But that's ridiculous. This is *Tony*.

"And you weren't even going to tell me, were you?" He asks in that deep, controlled tone, now tinted with accusation. "You summoned it without telling me, and you were just going to keep it hidden. Were you even planning on being there tomorrow night?"

"Of course I was," I reply in a small voice, looking down at my feet. "I still haven't made up my mind about—"

Without warning, Tony's hand flies towards me. He grabs my chin roughly, forcing me to look at him as he hunches down to meet me at eye level. His eyes are wide, wild, and burning.

"What did you just say?!" his voice is no longer steady and controlled. It is loud and demanding.

My breaths are shallow and fast. My heart threatens to explode out of the cage of my chest. I stare into his eyes, terrified, and feel the sting of tears making their way outward. His grip on my chin is making my jaw ache, pinching my skin. Out of the corner of my eye, I see that all of my plants are shaking violently like they are in an earthquake. Leaves, branches, and fronds all reach in my direction, but of course they can't reach me.

"Are you seriously still questioning this? This is who you are! This is what you are meant for! You are Persephone; you are *my* wife, *my* queen!"

Tony places his free hand on my arm, gripping my bicep firmly. He pushes me. I stumble backward, until I bump against one of my shelves. I feel green leaves and fronds poke the back of my neck and arms, reaching out for me. I feel them drying on my skin, wilting under me.

Tony's voice is getting louder. "Are you saying you don't want this anymore? Are you too good for this?!"

The tickle at the back of my head intensifies. Suddenly, I am not in my greenhouse. I am in a dark palace of marble and stone. *Our* palace. Hades has his hand on my throat and lower jaw, his face in mine, eyes blazing with rage. He is screaming at me, spittle flying from his mouth, but in my memory, there is no sound coming from his mouth.

The door to the greenhouse flies open. Tony's face goes slack, all traces of rage gone, and I see his focus shift down to where his hands are placed. For a fraction of a second, his eyes go wide with shock, and I see him yank his hands back to himself. He steps back in a flash, his face turning towards the door.

I, still stunned by what just happened, feel like I am moving in slow motion. I turn my head and see that Mom is out here, standing in the greenhouse doorway. She is frozen, stiff, with her hand still on the handle and her lips in a tight line. Her eyes flit back and forth between Tony and me. All around me, the plants' healthy green color restores slowly enough that I am the only one who notices. Leaves that had just been wilting grow firm again at the sight of my mom's presence, like they, too, can breathe again.

I look back at Tony, now across the length of the greenhouse from me. His face is turned downward, but he looks up at my mom with his eyes. He has his hands in his pockets in an attempt to look casual. Despite obvious guilt at being caught doing something he wasn't supposed to be doing etched all over him, he looks more like himself now than he has in weeks. Certainly, more than he did just seconds ago as he was getting in my face, rough-handling me.

What the hell just happened? I wonder.

"Tulip?" Mom's voice pierces the tension.

I look back at her. Her eyes are fully trained on Tony, glaring daggers at him.

"Everything okay out here?" she asks. Her tone is cool and even, a warning thinly veiled.

I let out a shaky breath. "Yeah," I say, "Tony was just about to leave."

I look back at Tony, who is still in that forced casual stance, his gaze still on my mom. For a second, I think he might try to return her stare-down. But, after a beat, he cuts his eyes to me for a split second and then walks toward the door.

My mom, one hand still on the door handle and the other on her hip, her chest puffed out, stays firmly in place, forcing Tony to stop in front of her so she can continue staring into his soul. Tony has a few inches on her, but looking at the two of them now, she seems to tower over him.

"Excuse me, Mrs. Burns." Tony mumbles.

"Let me make one thing clear to you, Anthony Jackson," Mom says in that too-calm tone, "if I ever catch you putting your hands on my daughter like that again, you are gonna answer to me."

I see Tony's jaw flex, but he says nothing.

Mom steps aside to let him leave, then watches him until he is out of sight, around to the front of the house.

At the sound of his car door shutting and the engine starting, Mom turns to look back at me.

"You know, you need a mask and a cape when you do that," I say.

Mom smirks, one eyebrow raised, "Left them in my secret cave." Then her face grows serious once again. "You okay?"

I take a deep breath, trying to steady myself. Am I okay?

"I will be," I tell her. "Thank you, Mom."

CHAPTER TWENTY-ONE

The smell of popcorn hangs in Val's room like a warm haze. On her parents' old TV, which sits on top of her large dresser, a psychological thriller from the 1990s plays on a low volume.

I'd almost forgotten how good it felt to talk to Val in our month of not speaking. We began the sleepover joking, laughing, and talking about how excited and nervous Val was to start on her college tennis team in just a couple of months.

As the afternoon started bleeding into the early evening, though, the tension inside me leaked outward.

Now, our attention is pulled to something aside from the TV glowing on the other side of the dresser.

My Chrysantheion fills Val's large room with its golden, shimmering light. It's like looking at a tiny sunset.

After school, Val had driven me home to grab my overnight bag and the flowerpot. Mom pulled into the driveway as I loaded them into Val's car, and when I hugged her goodbye for the night, I held onto her way longer than necessary, trying to commit to memory the way the embrace felt, acutely aware that it could be the last time I hugged my mom as her human, mortal daughter. The hug lasted so long that she chuckled uncomfortably and gave me two pats on the shoulder. When I still didn't let go, she pried herself away, completely unaware of the storm raging inside me.

Val lies on her stomach beside me as I sit cross-legged at the foot of her bed. She shoots me a wary, uncertain look.

"Do you want to go through the pros and cons again?" she asks.

I sigh. "I think we've beaten that poor dead horse enough. Thanks, though."

She rolls onto her side to face me, leaning on her elbow. "I wish I knew what to say to help."

"You and me both," I say, glancing at her quickly, forcing a smile. "I think I'm officially in over my head here. We are sitting across from my literal destiny. It feels... Like... Way too much, you know?"

"If you really feel like it's your destiny, then what's the hang-up?" Val asks.

"I don't know," I groan, standing from the bed and pacing around the room, running my hands through my hair and down my face.

"I guess I just don't like the fact that everyone acts like the Nectar is some inevitable finish line. I mean, say I drink it, right? Then what? Boom—Persephone is back, Tulip is gone. Like flipping a switch. I'm not Tracy's daughter anymore. I'm not just a friend, or just a girl. I'm something else that faded away a *long* time ago. Something I still don't even fully remember. And what if

I actually *like* being Tulip? Guess that doesn't matter once I'm divine again... If it even matters now."

Two roads diverged in a wood, I think.

I stop pacing. The silence between us is so thick, I can practically hear the Chrysantheion humming. When I turn to look at Val, she is watching me with soft, sympathetic eyes. But somehow, that makes this whole situation feel worse, not better.

"I know, I'm a broken record," I say, letting out a bitter snort.

Val exhales through her nose, almost a laugh, but not quite. "You make it sound like drinking that stuff will make you vanish into thin air. But from what you told me, you'll still be here. Still *you*."

"Until I'm not," I grumble, "when I'm some goddess in a crown, making decisions for people who never asked me to. Maybe it won't even be the Nectar's fault, though. Tony isn't Tony anymore, and he hasn't even summoned his Chrysantheion."

My fingers drift to my chin and gently trace my

jawline, remembering the way his face contorted with rage in my greenhouse yesterday. His absence from school today was, for once, easier to face than *he* would have been.

"Hey now, you stop that," Val says, her voice firm. "You are not Tony. For one thing, he doesn't have any real friends—let alone someone like *me* in his corner to remind him of who he is. And that's sad for him, don't get me wrong, but he chose to lean into all of this. That doesn't have to be you."

I wrap my arms around myself, feeling a lump rising in my throat.

"Do you think I should do it, then?" I croak as I blink back tears.

Val rises to her feet and approaches me. She wraps her arms around me in a tight hug. Then she backs away, placing her hands on both of my shoulders and looks me square in the face.

"No clue. But whatever you go with, I've got your back."

I'm here. Sadie's text says.

I had to assume Tony wouldn't be driving me to meet with everyone tonight, so I sent her a message with Val's address, asking her to come get me when the time came for all of us to start gathering.

Val sleeps next to me in her bed, not having moved a muscle or made a single sound since she first dozed off hours ago. Val's superpower is her ability to sleep through anything, from fire alarms to my constant tossing and turning at every sleepover. Knowing I won't disturb her, I don't bother to sneak slowly as I get out of her bed and slip my shoes on.

I raise Val's window before I grab my Chrysantheion from on top of her dresser, thankful not only that her room is on the ground floor but that her dog had long ago busted the screen out of it, making my sneaking out significantly easier than it would be if I had to leave out the front door.

I slide the window mostly shut behind me, then

make my way to the road where Sadie's car waits for me.

Sadie offers me a warm smile as I slide into the passenger seat. Her eyes flit to the Chrysantheion, and her smile wavers for just a second before she turns her attention back to me.

"Ready?" she asks.

"As ready as I'll ever be, I guess."

Sadie shifts the car into drive, and we are on our way to meet Nyx and the others.

Neither of us say much on the way, other than Sadie making sure that the car's air conditioner was at an okay temperature for me, and me reassuring her that it was fine.

The drive seems to stretch on for hours. The entire time, my heart flutters wildly in my chest, my cheeks feeling painfully flushed, and my hands feeling clammy around the flowerpot. My breathing feels too loud and shaky. Self-consciously, I turn to stare out my window but notice that the heat radiating off my body is fogging it up, so I instead turn to stare down at my own reflection in the shimmering surface of the Nectar.

My reflection's brow is furrowed, the eyes blinking rapidly, nostrils flaring wide with each breath out. My hands are shaking, and the image of me vibrates. I grip the flowerpot tighter to try and steady it and force some slow, deep breaths. I have a ringing in my ears that seems to grow louder with every inhale. My vision narrows and my head starts to spin, so I close my eyes against the sensation and beg my body to feel anything else.

"We're here," Sadie tells me softly, slowing the car onto the rough shoulder.

I look up and see Tony's car several yards ahead of us on the unlit road. I feel my chest tighten even more and worry that I may throw up.

Sadie reaches over and gives my back a quick rub.

"It'll be okay, Tulip. Whatever happens, whatever you choose, it will be okay."

I look at Sadie in the dark car, feeling like I want

to sob as I look at her sympathetic smile in the glow of the Nectar.

God, I wish I could believe you. I want to tell her.

Instead, I nod silently and unbuckle, then exit the car with Sadie, doing the same.

As she comes around the front of the car to join me so we can begin hiking towards the clearing, I ask Sadie: "If you aren't going to do this, why did you come tonight?"

She puts her arm around my shoulder, and we walk together into the line of trees.

"I didn't have much of a choice. Nyx's summoning is strong tonight. Don't you feel it?"

I do feel it. I've felt it for the last hour or so. Not only the usual tickle, but a nagging pull so intense that I wouldn't have been able to ignore it if I tried.

"Even if that weren't the case, though," she continues, "I wouldn't let my girl face this alone."

She doesn't look at me, choosing instead to keep

her eyes trained on the ground as we step over roots and bumps and try to avoid stepping into holes, but she squeezes my shoulders tighter affectionately.

The tickle grows stronger as we approach what I know to be the clearing, and the pull starts to ease up a little bit, like we finally get a break now that we are obeying it. I hear everyone's voices through the last of the trees, punctuated by a booming laugh, either from Moros or Logan.

"Well, if it isn't Little Springtime," Nyx's velvety voice cuts through the chatter as Sadie and I come into view of the others. The circle of gods is quieted instantly, as if on command. She cuts her eyes to Sadie and adds, "And of course the Wheat Mother."

My eyes automatically seek Tony out amongst the others. He stands between Tatum and Logan, with his hands in his pockets. He keeps his eyes trained on Nyx instead of returning my gaze, as if intentionally pretending I'm not there.

She steps towards Sadie and me as we approach and join the circle. Her black combat boots whisper against the grass under her feet. The corners of her lips curl into a sharp smile. Her ice-blue eyes shoot to my Chrysantheion, and it's only then that the smile seems to touch them.

"Well," she breathes, looking into my eyes, "Let's get started then, shall we?"

CHAPTER TWENTY-TWO

Nyx turns from me to address us all, pacing our circle slowly like a tiger stalking its prey.

"Tonight is the night we take back the our power. You've felt, throughout your new lives, how hollow the world has become without us. The mortals forgot who built all of this for them, but some have begun awakening to it. Their awakening has brought back ours, and we will make the rest of them remember as well."

I look around the circle at the other awakened gods. The others track Nyx's movement as she delivers her speech.

Tony's mouth curls into a confident smirk, and he lifts his chin as Nyx continues to speak. His face projects the entitlement he feels to the power she promises.

Logan mirrors Tony's stance, but his confidence tips into cockiness as Nyx goes on. Seeing the way he puffs out his chest as he listens to her brings back glimpses of my memories of him before, when he was just Ares—all bravado and arrogance, but handsome in a rough, rugged way.

I blink the memories away. I can't afford to be distracted right now.

Tatum watches Nyx, but with mild disinterest. She stands with all her weight on one foot, the other leg bent out. Her arms are crossed over her stomach, her expression bored and impatient, as if she's counting down the minutes until this is done.

As my gaze moves toward Moros, standing taller than the rest of us and thicker with muscles than both Logan and Tony, I startle when I realize his gaze—complete with his golden, lightening-bug pupils—is already fixed on me. He hasn't bothered to hide his divinity amongst us tonight, but he isn't glowing like he was the night he drank from his Chrysantheion.

One corner of his mouth lifts in a sneer when our eyes meet. I shrink into myself, feeling caught, and turn my attention back to Nyx.

"You didn't deserve to fade," she continues, her voice as smooth as velvet as she glides around the circle, "you didn't deserve to be forgotten. You deserve so much more."

She lets the words hang in the air. Then, her lips curve into a smile, warm and deadly.

"And tonight, you'll have it. Tonight, we leave the past behind us. We move from what we once were and into what we *will* be. Together. No more fading. No more being forgotten. No more feeble, fleeting mortality. No more diminished, half-realized powers and gifts. We will step back into our full power. We will find those who await awakening. The world yearns for us already. It has been *waiting* for us. Can't you feel it?"

Nyx's gaze drifts to Sadie, to Moros, to Tatum, to

Logan, to Tony—one at a time, lingering just long enough for each to feel singled out. Chosen.

Her eyes land on me last, then drift down to my Chrysantheion. She steps closer, and the glow reflects in her eyes, like flickers of a new flame.

"Together," she breathes, "we will carve out something new for ourselves—a new way to reign. Olympus is gone. The old thrones are dust. We will build something stronger. Something better. You will rise higher than you've ever dreamed of in your new lives. You will be greater than you ever were in your old lives."

Two roads diverged in a wood, I think. The thought comes to mind so abruptly, that I flinch.

Seeing me startle, Nyx lifts her eyes to meet mine again and smiles. The smile is snake-like, and my insides coil.

She turns away from me and surveys the others again. She raises her eyebrows as if an idea just occurred to her.

"I know there was some… concern last time we met about Zeus not being back yet. Concern about how we could restore ourselves without our old king to rule us," Tatum glances at Sadie and me, one eyebrow raised, but turns her attention quickly back to Nyx to avoid her noticing as she continues talking.

"It was a valid concern, of course. We *will* have to have some kind of pecking order. A guiding hand was always necessary to maintain our balance. The right leader will help us keep our power this time. Of course, I would never ask anyone here to take on that kind of responsibility. I couldn't possibly put that on any of you. I am willing to take up that mantle for us."

At this, I see Tatum roll her eyes hard and silently mime a gag.

If Nyx sees her, she ignores it. Instead, she smiles at each of us, again pausing for a few seconds as she looks around. Then, without warning, she claps her hands together once.

"And with that," she declares, "let's begin, shall we?"

There is a beat before anyone makes a move. I see Moros looking at the others, his arms crossed over his broad chest like a bouncer. His face is stern. He waits.

Logan is the first to move. He pulls a pocketknife out of his back pocket and, in an instant, slashes a clean line of crimson into his forearm. I gasp and turn my face away, but I hear the thick drops of blood splatter on the ground.

Out of the corner of my eye, I see Tony and Tatum move to perform similar acts of sacrifice—Tatum using a pair of shears she must have pulled out of her pocket, and Tony reaching down to the ground and plucking something white from it... An animal bone, I think—and using their objects to offer blood to the earth.

Just like before, I feel the ground pulsating beneath my feet and feel something invisible being pulled out of me. Sadie and I look at one another. She suddenly looks like it's a struggle for her to breathe, and I can tell that she feels it again, too.

Slowly, golden light spreads across her

face—first from one angle, then another, then a third—until she looks bathed in the glow of a sunset.

Once all the others' Chrysantheions have bloomed, the pulling sensation finally lets up. I feel like I can breathe again and see a similar relief relaxing Sadie's features.

I turn to see Nyx and Moros watching as Tony, Logan, and Tatum all pluck their flowers from the ground and throw back their Nectar. Their faces are smug, smiling with their eyes wide.

I turn my gaze to Tony, who still has not looked at me even once since I arrived. He throws the flower off to the side, discarding it like trash after he has drained the Nectar. He stands perfectly still, his eyes closed. The first change I notice is the cut he made on the palm of his hand knitting itself closed. Then light begins to fill his veins, shining so bright that I can see each intricately woven one through his skin. It looks like lava is cracking through the Earth.

His body stretches vertically, putting him at least a head taller than even Moros, then his shoulders broaden and stretch the fabric of his shirt to its limit. He opens his eyes—those gorgeous green eyes I've loved ever since we were small—and they are pitch black, just like in my memories.

My shoulders sink and my stomach drops at the sight of him. He still looks somewhat like Tony, but something about him now is… wrong. Uncanny. Too smooth. Too symmetrical.

Tatum too, transforms. It starts with her height, her body stretching until she looms over me like a tree. Her body's subtle curves become more pronounced. Her hair grows longer and thicker, reaching her waist. Her glow is subtle, as if really good stage lighting envelops her, the light comes from underneath her skin.

Logan's changes are the most drastic. Not only does he get taller than he already was, but his bulk becomes much more pronounced, his bicep and pectoral muscles busting the stitching of his T-shirt's sleeves, and his belly expanding underneath it. He doesn't look like a model or a movie star anymore, nor does he look like a bodybuilder with muscles designed purely for aesthetics.

He looks more like a professional boxer, whose body is made for fighting—solid as a rock.

The energy of their changes hums through the air, sharp and restless like an electric current. They all smile at one another, then at Nyx and Moros, both of whom look on proudly.

Nyx lets out a laugh of victory, clapping her hands together again.

But then she turns to look at me and Sadie, still mortal, and her smile turns to a look of confusion.

"Ladies," she says, her usual silky tone slipping, just for a moment, into the sharp edge of irritation. She pauses, seeming to collect herself, then tries again, "Ladies… Is there a problem?"

Sadie takes a shaky breath in, then steps forward, toward Nyx.

"I'm not reclaiming my divinity," she states, "I can't summon a Chrysantheion. Or maybe I can. I don't know. I haven't even tried."

Nyx's mouth pops open for just a second, but

then she snaps her teeth together and purses her lips. She looks Sadie up and down, from her feet and back to her face, slowly.

Then, she smirks. "Oh, sweet Wheat Mother," she says, "that's alright. Some of us just weren't meant to shine as brightly as the rest. You've been carrying the weight of mortality for so long—it's no wonder divinity feels so heavy to you."

Sadie scoffs but says nothing.

Nyx then turns her attention to me. She cocks her head to the side like a predator intrigued by its prey. I tighten my grip around the flowerpot, feeling the sweat from my palms slide over its surface.

"And you, Little Springtime? Clearly, you're more than capable of reclaiming your divinity. Your reign." She gestures to my Chrysantheion with both hands, her palms upward. "Why do you hesitate? Your husband has done what he needs to do. You don't want to be left behind by him, do you?"

She steps towards me. I jerk backwards, startled.

She brings her face close to mine, her cheek to my cheek, her lips nearly brushing against my ear.

"I know it's scary," she whispers in a voice dripping with honeyed tenderness so that only I can hear, "but you are ready, Tulip. This is what you're meant for. I know you better than anyone, and not just as Persephone. I know how hard things have been with your mom. With your friends. I know how much you have questioned your purpose your whole life. I know how much you want to do something meaningful. *This* is the ultimate purpose. The ultimate meaningful act. And what happens if you don't do this? You are the springtime. Mortals *need* you—and not just as one of them. I can't do this without you. Neither can he."

I glance over Nyx's shoulder to Tony—Hades and see him turn his radiant, unsettling face towards me for the first time since I arrived here tonight. My chest tightens at the sight of his new onyx eyes.

We share a look for just a second. In that second, I feel my eyes fill with tears. He looks away, towards the ground.

Two roads diverged in a wood.

I look back at Nyx as she takes a step back from me. When she sees my face, her eyes narrow slowly. Her face darkens.

I gulp. Then, I lean down and place the flowerpot on a level spot on the ground next to my feet. I raise myself up and square my shoulders, trying to come across as more self-assured than I feel.

When I speak, my voice is soft. Shaky.

"Nyx, I... I don't know if I'm ready to commit to—"

Nyx cuts me off, "Let's try this again," she says, raising her hand toward me, palm first, in an arch.

And then the entire world goes pitch black.

CHAPTER TWENTY-THREE

I am blind.

"WHAT HAVE YOU DONE TO ME?!" I cry out, clawing at my face desperately.

"NYX!" shouts a voice—Tony's voice, I think, followed by heavy footfall, twigs snapping, and the sound of cracking, like two rocks crashing into one another. Then grunting.

Someone barks, "Back the hell off!" through what sounds like clenched teeth.

Another voice growls, "She's not hurting her! Back up!"

"What are you doing?! Stop it!" Tatum's voice rings out, richer than it was before.

I drop to my knees, still clawing at my eyes, trying to rip away whatever veil Nyx has put over them.

"Oh my god, Tulip!" Sadie's voice says in my ear, and I feel her gentle hand on my shoulder. Her touch tethers me to the world even as my panic spikes and my heart races in my chest.

"You self-important little brat!" Nyx's voice cuts through my panic as she spits her words at me. "Who exactly do you think you are? Who exactly do you think you're dealing with here?"

"Nyx, stop!" Sadie cries, then I feel her hand rip from my shoulder. The sounds of grunting and growling—the sounds of a struggle, of a fight—continue somewhere in front of me.

My head spins, trying to make sense of the chaos. I claw at my eyes, breath coming in jagged gasps.

Nothing. Only blackness.

I feel breath on my face, slow and even.

"You child," Nyx hisses at me, "do you really believe mortals need *flowers?* You mean nothing to them. It's him. He thinks he needs you. That he can't take on his old role without you. No matter how many discussions we've had, he thinks there can be no Hades without his Persephone. Do you really think you have a choice? I offer you purpose, power, and control over your own fate, and you really think there's an option to say no to that? To say no to *me?* I'm not just a goddess; I am the night! You don't get to say no to the night, little girl. You are going to take your Nectar. You are going to let go of these childish fantasies that mortal life has some kind of meaning and beauty. Grow up and do your job."

"NYX, *PLEASE*, I CAN'T SEE!" I sob.

I hear her let out a bitter snort.

"Now there's the understatement of the century." She hisses.

The heat of her breath no longer warms my face.

When she speaks next, her voice comes from above me. It is deeper and more acidic than I have ever heard it.

"I'm not like the rest of you. I never faded. I was old before your idiot father, and your soft husband ever came into being. I was ancient before Olympus was ever even dreamt of. I am older than the very first break of dawn. I will not be refused by a scared little flower. I do not beg. I do not wait. I take."

I hear the scuffling coming closer. Curses fly from mouths faster than I can register them.

I hear Sadie groaning nearby, sounding disoriented and foggy.

I hear my own screaming sobs and panicked gasps.

I hear laughter coming from above me. Icy and cruel and smug.

Every part of my body hurts, my muscles wracked from the strain and force of my desperate sobs. My chest tightens so painfully that I'm sure it's collapsed in on itself. Bile rises in my throat, and I choke on it.

And then, without warning, I am in a field of wildflowers.

The sounds of the chaos around me have vanished.

Whatever magic Nyx put over my eyes to plunge me into darkness is gone.

At the snap of a finger, I am thrust into the past.

Into a memory.

I sit on the ground amongst the flowers, my legs tucked under me. My mother, Demeter, sits behind me. She runs her fingers through my long hair, the color of sun-kissed amber. She intricately braids while I talk in our ancient language.

"I just don't know what my role is there, Mother," I say, "I am Spring. That is why he loves me. That is why he chose me for his wife. How am I to be Spring—the deliverer of new life—in a place with no life?

Mother chuckles, "You don't mold the head to wear the crown, my blossom. You mold the crown to fit the head."

I pull away and turn back to look at her, confused. "Meaning?"

Mother smiles, her eyes soft and warm, "You are trying to force yourself to fit into a role that has never existed before you. You are the one who will determine the role and what it entails. You are the one who will dictate how you can be both Spring and Queen of the Underworld."

"That's the problem," I groan before relaxing back into her hair braiding, "I don't know how. They are opposites. Two conflicting sides. Am I to be both life and death? How can one be both? What am I supposed to be, Mother?"

She wraps her arms around me from behind and places her chin on my shoulder.

"You are supposed to be *you*, my blossom," she says warmly, giving my arms a squeeze for emphasis.

"But what am I?" I ask in a whisper petulantly.

Mother tightens her arms around me and begins rocking me side to side, like she would when I was small.

"My sweet daughter, you keep trying to split yourself in two—as though you are one creature in the sunlight, and another in the dark. But you are not divided. You are whole. You walk both paths at once, because you can. Two roads may diverge, but you are the one who binds them. The gods and the earth do not choose between seed and harvest, or between death and bloom. Both belong. So it is with you."

Chaos surrounds me again.

I am thrust back into my current reality. Back into darkness.

"Tulip?" Sadie moans from somewhere off to my side, her tongue sounding thick in her mouth.

"PERSEPHONE!" Tony calls out from far away, shouting over the sound of heavy breathing and growling, and violence.

Two roads diverged in a wood, and I—I took the one less traveled by.

Memories flash quickly through my mind like a slideshow. Despite the blackness of whatever Nyx has done to me, I can see them with perfect clarity.

My mother embracing me as Persephone.

Being embraced by Hades as I faded.

Opening my eyes for the first time as Tulip Lorelai Burns, seeing the faces of my parents come into focus. Dad's tears spilling over his wide smile. Mom's sweaty, tear-stained face bringing me to her lips to kiss my little forehead.

Tony and I, running on the playground the day we met, dodging the swings and pretending they were wrecking balls in an obstacle course.

Laughing hysterically with Val as we tried taping the lemon-flavored candy to the poster board my mom had picked up at the store that morning, the day our presentation on the candy was due.

Meeting Laura.

Meeting Steph.

Meeting Reagan and Alondra.

Tony. Kissing Tony in his car. Kissing Tony in the halls at school, knowing we were gods but still feeling like children.

Dad running ahead of me up the steps of the waterslide. Looking back at me, laughing.

Dad getting sick.

Dad dying.

Mom holding me in the kitchen.

Sadie squeezing my shoulder.

I place my palms on the ground in front of me, digging my fingers into the earth. I let out my breath, ridding my lungs of their last sobs, then take a slow, intentional breath in through my nose.

I am not Persephone. I am also not just Tulip. I am both. I always have been. Tony chose to be Hades alone, but I was never meant to split myself. I was always the bridge. My road was never the well-worn one or the less traveled one... It's the one no one has dared to make before me. It's the path that *no one* has walked before.

I push my hands into the dirt, like a lion bracing itself for a roar.

Nyx's cruel laughter continues above me. The chaos still surrounds me.

I breathe out slowly through my mouth, my lips puckered into a small circle. As my breath leaves my body, I feel my energy penetrate the soil below my hands. I push it down, down, down into the ground, letting it take root.

Then, just as I had pushed my energy into the earth, I began to pull from deep within it, drawing energy from it. I take another slow, deep breath in and tug at the energy, like I'm pulling water up from a well. I pull it into myself. I let it fill me up.

Then, cracks in the blackness that surround me begin to form. They shine bright green and gold through this veil until all the blackness shatters, and I can see.

I gasp and turn my head to my left, where Sadie is pulling herself into a seated position on the ground, touching the back of her head.

I turn to look past Nyx, who stands towering over me, and see Tony struggling against Moros and Logan, who each hold him by an arm. Tatum is trying to pry Logan's fingers off Tony.

Nyx's laughter fades to a halt over me.

Tony stops struggling, his eyes wide as he lays them on me. Even Moros, Tatum, and Logan freeze and look at us.

I take a second to steady myself, then slowly rise to my feet.

I rise until I am eye-level with Nyx. I stare into her eyes. Her mouth is a snarl, but her eyes are widened slightly in surprise.

I wipe the back of my hand under my eyes, swiping away the last of my tears. Not breaking eye contact with Nyx, I turn my face to the side and spit bile to the ground. Then, I turn fully back to her.

She breathes hard, her fists clenched tightly to her sides. She is vibrating with the effort of not shaking in rage. Her pale face hardens with it as her eyes grow glassy, staring into mine.

"No one says no to the night, huh?" I ask, my voice low and shockingly steady. My insides tremble so hard that I feel like I'm buzzing. "And yet... I just did."

Nyx staggers back like I hit her, now shaking violently. A single tear, shimmering and golden, slides down her cheek.

"Thousands of years," she says to me, her voice quavering ungracefully, "thousands of years, I've been alone. Do you—" her voice breaks, sincere for maybe the first time since I've met her, "do you have any idea what that's like?"

My stomach sinks, but I say nothing, only hold her gaze as she takes another step back.

Her face hardens. The look she gives me is full of venom and loathing. Whatever vulnerability that just bled through is gone.

"You disappoint me," she spits.

Then, she turns to the others—Moros, Logan, Tatum, and Tony—and barks, "Let's go."

One by one, the gods led by Nyx exit the clearing. Tony is the last to leave. He stands across from me, staring at me. His expression is mostly blank. Only his eyes, wide under a slightly knitted brow, reveal any trace of sadness.

Eventually, he turns his back on me and follows the rest of them. His steps drag, but he goes, nonetheless.

And then—nothing.

The sudden silence in the clearing is jarring after all the chaos. Even the crickets seem to be holding their breath. My ears ring in the heavy, unreal silence.

I stay rooted in place for a moment, afraid that any sudden movement will make me collapse.

Eventually, I turn and go to Sadie, who is still sitting on the ground, her eyes looking foggy and unfocused. I crouch next to her and help her to her feet, keeping my hand on her arm to steady her.

317

"Are you okay?" she asks me, her words dragging as they come out.

I raise an eyebrow at her. "I think I should be asking you that."

She tilts her head at me, her eyes becoming misty and her mouth pressing into a flat line.

"You were incredible," she rasps.

My heart swells in my chest. I look away from her and see my Chrysantheion, still in its flowerpot, standing flat on the ground. I step toward it and pick it up in one hand before coming back to hook Sadie's arm over my other shoulder.

"Come on," I say, "let's get out of here."

CHAPTER TWENTY-FOUR

I glide towards the mirror at the end of the hallway.

In it, I see myself dressed in a soft green, floor-length tulle gown. The V-neck plunges far lower than anything I've ever dared to wear before, while thin sleeves drape gracefully over my shoulders and flutter like butterfly wings. Golden yellow, dusty rose, and lavender embroidered flowers wind through the layers of tulle, their stems swirling like vines.

My hair is braided into a crown with a few curled locks hanging down tastefully, tickling my shoulders.

Baby's breath clippings peek through my braid, stark white against copper.

My eyes are lined with brown, my eyelashes looking thick and extra long with mascara. My eyeshadow is a shimmery design not unlike a butterfly's wings, done in the colors of the flowers on my dress. My lips are stained a matte, mauve pink. I look more beautiful than I think I ever have before, but I still feel like *me*.

Val comes up behind me and drapes her arm over my shoulders. Her burgundy, off-the-shoulder, A-line dress, slit high up her thigh, making her look like a bombshell. Her thick, raven hair tumbles loose, framing her tan shoulders.

In the mirror, she winks one of her black winged-lined eyes at me and says, "Our parents are nagging us for pictures before we leave. You ready?"

I smile at her reflection. "Let's do this!"

We turn away from the mirror at the end of her parents' hallway and make our way back to the living room where her parents and my mom wait with their phones already up, ready to snap a billion candid and posed shots of us.

"Smile, girls, it's your prom night!" Val's mom cheers from her spot in the middle of the room, already furiously tapping her finger on the photo button on her screen as we walk out to meet them.

"Mom, ay, *Dios*," Val laughs, rolling her eyes.

"She's right, Val! I need to see some pearly whites!" My mom says, also tapping her phone screen like it's a race.

I laugh too, and Val and I allow our parents to direct us through a series of poses inside the house, outside the house in the back yard, by Val's car, by Val's dad's motorcycle, by the neighbor's crepe myrtle, and on and on until Val says: "Okay, parents! If we don't go now, we're gonna miss the whole prom!"

Our school always holds the prom at a country club in town. The parking lot is already full by the time we arrive at sunset, so Val joins a line of lifted trucks that have parked in the grass. We lock her car and walk inside with our arms linked, the bass from the music rattling my ribs before we are even all the way across the parking lot. As we approach the entrance, I run the fingers of my free hand over the yellowing leaves of the bushes that line the patio, smiling as they turn a vibrant green under my touch and reach their thin branches out after me as I pass by.

We spot Alondra, Laura, and Reagan at a table and quickly go to join them. All three look stunning in their dresses, though Laura's discomfort is obvious in the way she slouches her shoulders.

Alondra stands, greeting us with a smile as soon as she sees us. She hugs me, then backs away to look me up and down.

"You look so pretty!" she cries out over the loud music.

"Me? Look at *you*!" I shout back. She wears a dark purple sleeveless ballgown-style dress. She looks like a princess in the best way.

I turn to Laura and Reagan, who wear matching spaghetti strap silk gowns, Laura's in black and Reagan's in red.

"You guys look awesome!" I shout over the music.

Laura allows her lips to quirk up a little in a small smile.

"Thanks," she shouts, "you too!"

"Where's Stephanie?" Val shouts.

Reagan rolls her eyes but laughs as she does so. "Oh, she's on the dance floor." She replies.

Val and I look toward the dance floor and, sure enough, see Steph grinding on a junior boy in her short, sleeveless, royal blue bubble cocktail dress. We exchange a look and laugh, then join our friends at the table, ready for whatever tonight brings.

We eat catered finger foods. We dance to all the best, cheesiest, fastest songs. We laugh, we reminisce about our high school memories, and we reiterate plans to visit one another next year on breaks. I inform everyone—other than Val, who was the first person I told after deciding with my mom—that I will be going to Everhart University, a college six hours away, and the only one in the state that offers a Music Business program.

I get cheers and hugs and congratulations from all my friends. My heart swells. I look around at all their faces and try to soak in every detail. I never want to forget this night, and how it feels being here with them. It feels so fleeting, this night with all its beautiful moments, that it makes every second feel precious.

I let my gaze float around the ballroom, taking in the whole setting. Suddenly, I feel the tickle at the back of my mind and the hair on my arms stands on end. I whip my head around, searching across the room until I see him.

Tony. Standing in a doorway that leads outside, to the country club's garden, dressed in an all-black suit.

Our eyes meet across the dance floor. Then, he turns and walks slowly out the door.

"I'll be right back," I shout to my friends before rising from the table and making a beeline to that door.

I exit the building, leaving behind the ear-splitting music and flashing lights and the smell of sweat and body spray for the smell of summer flowers and wet grass.

The garden is beautiful; rows of flowers and small shrubs are arranged around a lantern-lit path that leads to a white gazebo that looks out onto a vast golf course, with fairy lights strung up from the ceiling.

Tony stands in the gazebo, his back to me, hands in his pockets. I hike up the skirt of my gown, revealing the dusty rose-colored low-top Converse I wear under my dress, and make my way to him.

When I reach the gazebo, I hear the music from inside trickling down from overhead. I look up to see a white painted speaker attached to the ceiling. I look back at Tony as he turns to face me. I have to stop myself from gasping when I see him up close.

"You look…" I sputter, struggling to fill in the

blank. *You look right. You look mortal. You look like* you.

"You look handsome." I finally say.

It's true. He cleans up very nicely. He is clearly disguised as his old, mortal self— shorter than he was after he drank his Nectar and reclaimed his divinity, not as broad in the shoulders as he became... he even has his agate-green eyes back. I feel tears form in my eyes at the sight of them. I swallow, choking them back.

He smiles softly and lets his glassy eyes drift over me from head to toe, lingering at some more attention-grabbing parts.

"You look incredible," he says softly.

I smile back at him and fiddle with the skirt of my dress. Over our heads, a fast, techno song changes to a slow ballad.

Tony reaches a hand out to me, palm up.

"May I have this dance?" he asks.

I slide my hand into his and allow him to pull me close. He wraps his other arm around my waist. I place mine on his shoulder. He leads, swaying our bodies from side to side across the floor of the gazebo.

We say nothing for a while, just looking into one another's eyes. I wonder if he, like me, is trying to pretend that there is nothing at all unusual about this moment. We are just a boy and a girl at their senior prom.

Tony is the one to break the silence between us.

"Tulip, I owe you an apology," he says. I notice that he doesn't call me by my old name for the first time since my awakening. It feels both like a sigh of relief and a painful sting.

He continues: "For that day, in your greenhouse. I... I can't believe I put my hands on you like that. I don't know—"

I shake my head, cutting him off. "You weren't *you*."

"That's the thing, though. I think I was. That is what scares me about it. I did it without thinking. I did it so naturally. It was basically second nature. I saw myself doing it to you before… In our old lives."

I swallow hard. I know that we are thinking of the same memory, somehow. The one I saw glimpses of on that day.

"I never want to do that again," he declares. "I can't be that way… I won't let myself. I promise you, I will never do anything to hurt you ever again."

I blink up at him, but I say nothing. We continue to sway.

Tony clears his throat. "So, what happened to your Chrysantheion after we left?"

I take in a quick breath, sharply. "I, uh, took it home. I put it back in the greenhouse, after I made sure Sadie got home. I guess Nyx hit her in the head pretty hard… I had to wake up her husband and make sure she was okay."

He nods. "Is she? Okay, I mean."

"Yeah," I say breezily, "she had a mild concussion. But she's good now."

He nods again, then looks away and sucks in his lips, still nodding occasionally in thought. He does this for a long time.

"You aren't going to drink your Nectar, are you?" he says. He phrases it like a question, but there is no uncertainty in his tone. This is not a question, but confirmation.

I keep my eyes on him for a beat, studying his face, which is still not turned back to me. I want to remember it just like this. I want to remember his beautiful green eyes. I want to remember the warm hue of his skin, the bounce of his curls. I want to remember the way his cologne smells.

So, I decide not to confide in him how I've been going into my greenhouse at least twice a day just to hold my Chrysantheion and stare into the shimmering Nectar. I decide to study his face as it is now, while he's disguised as a mortal, and hope that it doesn't get erased by all the memories of his old face that keep coming back to me, or the memory of his new divine face as it was that night in the clearing. I decide to keep all of that to myself so that, at least for the moment, I can be just a girl who loves him, and he can be just a boy who loves me back.

I let out a sigh and lower my head to rest on his chest, moving my hands so that my arms snake up through his arms, to the back of his shoulders. I listen for his heartbeat, but I hear nothing. Immortal gods don't have human hearts.

"I'm not," I say, lifting my face to look at his again, "at least not *now*. Maybe not ever… But… Definitely not now."

He nods again, then finally lowers his face to look at me. His eyes shine in the fairy lights. Pain is etched across his face.

I feel the tickle at the back of my head again, and glance past his shoulder, across the golf course. There is a tree line there, and at the edge of the tree line stands the others—the gods who reclaimed their divinity, not bothering to disguise themselves—and Nyx.

"I guess that's your cue to leave," I say sadly as I

look back up at him.

We stop swaying, and he takes a step back from me. He looks me over one more time, then reaches forward to cup my face with both of his hands. He bends down to plant his lips on mine in a passionate, desperate kiss. I realize that he wants to remember this, just like I do.

When we eventually part, he places his forehead against mine. His eyes are closed. I watch as a single golden tear slides down his cheek. This breaks me, and I feel my own tears cross the barriers of my lower lids and drip down from my jawline.

Tony lets out a single, wet, shaky breath.

"I will love you forever," he murmurs.

Above us, the ballad slows to a stop and transitions to a new song. The fairy lights sway in a gentle breeze.

And then he stands up straight, turns away from me and walks off toward whatever his endless future is, leaving me on uncharted ground to carve out my own way.

EPILOGUE

Waves crashed against the rocky shore. Elliot
Mariner—yes, his name *is* perfect for someone who
works at a lighthouse museum, thank you for
noticing—sat alone on the dock and waited for the water
taxi to come pick him up and take him to his car on the
mainland for the evening.

It had been a long day of repeating the same
anecdotes about the historical lighthouse to countless
tourists. He'd answered the same questions thousands of
times, tried to ignore the whining of the tourists'
children, begging their parents to take them somewhere

that was actually fun, and still maintained the cheerful smile that was expected of a Visitor Services Associate. Now, all Elliot wanted in the whole world was to get back to his one-bedroom apartment, heat up some instant ramen, turn on American Dad and turn off his brain until he had to wake up and do it all again in the morning.

Elliot was 28 years old, but his body ached like a much older man. Before Stella dumped him, he could sometimes sweet-talk her into giving him a back rub until he fell asleep so that he didn't spend the first hours of lying in bed tossing and turning, trying to get comfortable. But then, Stella started dropping hints about their future, texting him pictures of engagement rings that she liked and links to house listings in the suburbs, and he recoiled so harshly at her obvious fishing that he became someone even he barely recognized. And that was the end of that.

Now, he lived alone again for the first time since college and worked at this old, mildew-scented lighthouse, giving annoying, sunburnt tourists in their wide-brimmed hats the same spiels about the history of the lighthouse and whaling on the coast again and again, and waited—not without bitterness—for his life to start.

As Elliot trained his eyes on the horizon, he didn't notice at first that the surface of the water directly in front of the dock started to bubble. It wasn't until the bubbles came faster and larger, like the water was boiling, that it finally grabbed his attention.

He jumped to his feet and peered over the edge of the dock, his mouth hanging open.

"What the hell?" he said to himself.

Suddenly, a large mass of dark greens—the color of mold and mud and seaweed—with a dark brown line running straight up the middle emerged amongst the bubbles.

It continued to rise from the water. At first, Elliot thought that maybe this was some kind of boulder, or a large, deformed clam. But, as the mass continued to rise from the water, Elliot's eyes widened in horror, trying desperately to make sense of what he was seeing.

It was a head... A giant head, coming out of the

water. The face alone was the size of Elliot's flatscreen TV. It continued to rise, revealing the naked torso of a giant man. His hair was long and dark green, with streaks of sea foam sliding through it as it fell down his back. His thick beard was the same color as his hair, and dripped ocean water as he rose. His skin was deeply tanned but had a sheen of silvery blue iridescence that shone in the setting sun. His chest and shoulders were broad and muscular, the kind of build that the girls Elliot had spent his teen years chasing preferred to his own lanky build.

The giant man stepped forward through the sea toward the lighthouse. As he did so, Elliot let out a gasped cry—not really a word so much as a sound.

This seemed to catch the giant man's notice. He turned his face and those dark, ocean-blue eyes towards Elliot and bent forward at the waist to get a better look.

Elliot fell backwards and started crab-walking to put as much distance between himself and the giant man, still making the sounds of awe and horror, yet unable to peel his eyes away from the sight of him.

The giant man smirked, seeming entertained by Elliot's fear. Then, he reached forward and scooped Elliot up in one of his massive hands.

It was then that Elliot began to scream, as the giant man stood up straight and brought his hand with Elliot in it close to his face, like he was studying a bug specimen.

Elliot screamed until his voice was raw, his throat feeling torn apart by his own voice. Tears streamed down his face.

Then, with no effort whatsoever, the giant man tossed Elliot over his shoulder like a crumpled-up piece of paper.

The last thing Elliot saw was the sea rushing towards him as his arms and legs thrashed wildly.

ACKNOWLEDGEMENTS

This book would not have been completed without the constant support of my husband and soulmate, Daniel. The gratitude I feel for the countless hours he spent proofreading each chapter as I finished it—and for giving me immediate feedback to help make Awaken Persephone the best it could possibly be—is something I can never fully express… but I will never stop trying.

I also owe so much to Jenny—my Val—for her

constant encouragement and support. She's the sun energy to my moon energy and my hetero-lifemate. Tulip and Val's friendship wouldn't have the same sparkle if it weren't for the friendship we share. So, thank you, Jen! And thank you to Lemonheads for bringing us together in 7th-grade Pre-AP English!

I am so incredibly lucky to have a village of talented women in my life. Kelcey, the amazing artist and creative spirit who brought my vision for the book cover to life and took my author photos, somehow managed to make me look less like a big toe. I don't know how she did that, but dang... it was impressive! Dr. Phoebe Hayes, my teacher certification program buddy, is the amazing editor to whom I owe probably the most gratitude—for meticulously combing through every word and ensuring that everything in this book makes sense.

Though I don't know him personally (I sure wish I did), I owe a debt of gratitude to Hozier for creating the music that always put me in the right headspace to write. Every scene in the greenhouse is accompanied by a

Hozier song in the soundtrack inside my head. So thank you, Hozier, for your soothing, botanical vibes and the velvety voice you've deemed us mere mortals worthy to hear.

To the kids I taught—though I suppose y'all aren't really kids anymore—in freshman English at GHS: thank you for inspiring me with your creative minds and for letting me watch how you exist in your unique worlds. I couldn't have written this book without the many ways you all inspired me. I loved watching the way your minds worked and will never stop being proud of you. You are forever my Precious Little Pomegranates.

Lastly, to all the women in my life who helped shape me into the woman I am—Nana, Mom, Haley, Mrs. Anderson, Mrs. Bradshaw, Cookie, all the women I've already mentioned, and of course my babies, Diana and Leia, and the people you'll become someday—thank you. This book is a love letter to you and to the relationships I have with each of you. You give me a strength that feels almost otherworldly. You are all goddesses.